"You don't have to worry," Costa blithely continued. "I loathe PDAs, so I shan't be all over you. We would dance of course, and they would expect that we kiss now and then, but that would be all."

"And no sex?"

"I didn't say that." He looked right at her then, and the look he gave was so potent it stripped her. Not just her clothes, for she felt translucent, as if he could see right inside, witnessing her tightening desire.

"I'm not sure I know what you mean?" Mary croaked.

"Then I'll make it very clear—apart from when we have an audience present, I shan't lay a finger on you."

"And when they're not present?"

"The same," Costa said. "You either want me or you don't."

"If I don't?"

"I have a guest suite in my villa." Costa shrugged.

"And, if..." She felt a little giddy, a little baffled that she could even attempt to say what she was about to. "If I do want you?"

"Then you come to me."

Carol Marinelli

THE GREEK'S
CINDERELLA DEAL

HARLEQUIN
PRESENTS

ISBN-13: 978-1-335-56907-3

The Greek's Cinderella Deal

Copyright © 2021 by Carol Marinelli

Recycling programs
for this product may
not exist in your area.

This edition published by arrangement with Harlequin Books S.A.

For questions and comments about the quality of this book,
please contact us at CustomerService@Harlequin.com.

Harlequin Enterprises ULC
22 Adelaide St. West, 40th Floor
Toronto, Ontario M5H 4E3, Canada
www.Harlequin.com

Printed in U.S.A.

Carol Marinelli recently filled in a form asking for her job title. Thrilled to be able to put down her answer, she put "writer." Then it asked what Carol did for relaxation and she put down the truth—"writing." The third question asked for her hobbies. Well, not wanting to look obsessed, she crossed her fingers and answered "swimming"—but, given that the chlorine in the pool does terrible things to her highlights, I'm sure you can guess the real answer!

Books by Carol Marinelli

Harlequin Presents

Secret Prince's Christmas Seduction

One Night with Consequences

The Sicilian's Surprise Love-Child

Secret Heirs of Billionaires

Claiming His Hidden Heir
Claimed for the Sheikh's Shock Son

The Ruthless Deveraux Brothers

The Innocent's Shock Pregnancy
The Billionaire's Christmas Cinderella

Those Notorious Romanos

Italy's Most Scandalous Virgin
The Italian's Forbidden Virgin

Visit the Author Profile page
at Harlequin.com for more titles.

PROLOGUE

'WE NEED TO TALK.'

Costa Leventis barely looked up from his computer as Galen approached. 'Not now.'

It was Saturday morning, but the day of the week stopped neither working and Costa really wanted to get on. Yet Galen wasn't budging.

'Why do you still not have a PA?'

'Why would I when I can borrow yours?'

It was both a running joke and a bone of contention—they shared a vast office space in Kolonaki, an upmarket neighbourhood in Athens. Or rather Galen's tech company was run from the same building as Costa's property empire.

At first they had combined their limited resources for what had been practically a cupboard in the affluent neighbourhood. Their smart address had made their ventures more believable to the powers that be. They were not friends as such—just two poor boys from Anapliró who wanted to do well. For themselves rather than for each other. Their arrangement had worked, for between them they now jointly owned the building and separately each owned much more.

'Your borrowing my PA is the reason we need to speak,' Galen said. 'Kristina will be going on maternity leave soon—'

'Is she expecting, then?'

'Jesus, Costa!' Galen couldn't help but give a reluctant laugh. 'She's nearly seven months.'

'Well, if you're hiring a new PA, could I suggest you get one with a warmer personality?'

'I'm not asking for advice,' Galen countered. 'Kristina and I have been discussing what her job will look like on her return and you're the main sticking point. She loathes running your extensive little black book.'

'Please,' Costa dismissed. 'Occasionally I might ask her to send flowers, or cancel a restaurant booking.'

'You've just called her at home, on a Saturday morning, and asked her to sort out a flight, book your preferred London hotel and organise a private table at the bar.'

'It was a last-minute decision. Anyway, that's business and nothing to do with my little black book.'

'Kristina deals with *my* business. She's not on *your* payroll.'

Both men were formidable in their own way, and neither was prone to backing down.

'You need to hire your own PA, not constantly

borrow mine. You have damned virtual assistants everywhere, yet no single point of contact.'

'*I* am my point of contact,' Costa said.

He certainly didn't want someone delving into his business and knowing his whereabouts, but more to the point…

'Hey, for all I'm suddenly the bad guy, why wasn't Kristina having the same issues with me when she was trying to find a location for her engagement party?'

Costa answered Galen's silence.

'It was held in my hotel in Paris and, if I remember correctly, I covered the bill. Then, when she told you she was considering leaving work because of the stress of her wedding, compounded by Difficult Me, didn't I tell her my staff in Liechtenstein would take care of her wedding?'

Yes, Costa might ask for her help on occasion, but she was extremely well compensated for her occasional reluctant efforts.

'She has another agenda,' Costa stated, for while Galen was better with numbers, Costa was an expert at reading people.

'Just stop asking her to take care of your business.'

'For sure,' Costa said. 'I shall send flowers and apologise.'

Though he doubted that would appease Kristina; he was positive that she was after something.

'So what are you doing, meeting with Ridgemont now?' Galen asked.

Costa frowned, for Galen was not one for idle conversation. Certainly they rarely got involved in each other's line of work. 'I told Kristina not to gossip.'

'It was a formal complaint, not gossip,' Galen countered. 'It's signatures next week on the Middle East deal, isn't it?'

Costa didn't respond.

'I'm just curious as to why you're seeing him tonight when you've been stalling for weeks.'

'We're Greek,' Costa responded casually. 'You know that means we do business face to face.'

'Ridgemont's not Greek,' Galen needlessly pointed out. 'And you stopped partying with him long ago.'

'Some things are best said out of the boardroom.'

'Costa,' Galen warned. 'I'm not sure what you're up to, but—'

'Let's keep it that way.' Costa was brusque now, closing his computer and getting ready to head off to catch his plane.

'The recent land sale in Anapliró…the *unavoidable* delays…' Galen spoke on. 'If I'm guessing right, then so too might Ridgemont.'

Still Costa said nothing.

'He's a tyrant.'

'You think I don't know that?'

'Look, I don't doubt you have the legalities covered. But for all Ridgemont's pedigree he's a spoiled man-child with a temper. If you're about to shaft him…'

Christ, even *Galen* could see it!

'Then it's just as well I was once *kakoúrgos*.' Costa shrugged, for he had survived the streets and, yes, had been a bit thuggish at times. 'Don't waste your time worrying about my business.'

'Keep your guard up, Costa…' Galen warned.

Except Costa did not need Galen's warning. His guard had been up for more than a quarter of a century.

Costa had hated Eric Ridgemont with a passion since he was ten. Not that Galen or anyone else knew that.

Now he was headed to London with but one thing on his mind.

Severance.

It started tonight.

CHAPTER ONE

ONCE UPON A TIME she'd been brave. Mary had it in writing!

Lost in a daydream as she swept the salon floor, Mary thought of the old-school report she had leafed through last night.

Mary can be somewhat reckless at times...
Mary seems to delight in mischief...

Yes, and once she had worn a mettlesome smile and been full of daring and spirit...

'Mary!'

She was startled by the voice of Coral, her boss.

'I need to speak to you.'

'Of course!'

'In the staffroom.'

Mary leant the broom against the wall and wanted to quickly retie her rather tatty blonde hair because, though she feigned nonchalance, Mary was rather certain she knew what this was about. At least she hoped she did!

Today was her twenty-first birthday, and usually there was a little party held in the salon for birthdays and engagements and such.

Up until now the day had felt wretched—her birthday had gone unannounced and unnoticed. Even her father hadn't sent a card.

'You're not in trouble,' Coral added as they walked through the hair salon—perhaps because all too often Mary was.

Whatever went wrong in the rather shabby London salon, somehow it ended up being her fault. But now, just when she had given up hoping, things were looking up.

'Do you have plans for tonight?' Coral asked as they made their way through a cramped corridor out to the back.

'No, none,' Mary responded as hope flared higher. Maybe, finally, she was going to be invited out with 'the Saturday night crowd', as some of the staff called themselves. The popular staff, of which Mary wasn't one.

'That's good, because I've got a favour to ask,' Coral said, pushing the staffroom door open.

'A favour?' Mary checked, bracing herself for shouts of 'Happy birthday!' and preparing to act surprised. Anticipating balloons, and cake, and the pop of a champagne cork, even though Mary herself didn't drink.

Except the staffroom was empty and one glance

told her that there was no cake—just an awful lot of mugs she would have to wash up tonight.

'What sort of favour?' Mary asked, choking back disappointment while still clinging to the hope that they were going to celebrate her birthday after work.

'I've got a date tonight,' Coral said, 'and I can't wriggle out of it. Believe me, I've tried...'

Mary frowned.

'The thing is, Costa Leventis is flying in from Athens.' She looked at Mary's still bemused expression. 'Please don't tell me you haven't heard of him.'

'I haven't.'

Coral sighed with irritation. 'He's important—extremely important—and there's been a dinner arranged at short notice...' She named a very exclusive Mayfair hotel and Mary's eyes widened. 'The trouble is I already have a cli— I mean, a date tonight. I'm asking if you'll please step in.'

'To go on a date with Costa Le—?'

'Heavens, no!' Coral laughed at the very notion. 'Believe me, I'd drop anything for that. No, the dinner date is with Eric Ridgemont, who is meeting with Costa Leventis.'

Mary had no idea who he was either, but she blinked when Coral told her how much she'd be paid, for it was significantly more than she made in a week.

For going out to dinner.

Mary might be utterly innocent where men were concerned, but she wasn't naïve. Her time in and out of foster care as her father had drifted in and out of prison had taught her quite a lot about life. Coral's red sports car and designer wardrobe didn't exactly equate with a salon that wasn't doing particularly well.

'*Just* dinner?' Mary checked dubiously.

'Whatever you want,' Coral said. 'Look, I know it's short notice, but you've already said you don't have plans tonight.'

'I'm sorry.' Mary shook her head. 'No.'

'This is really important,' Coral warned.

Not to me, it isn't, Mary was tempted to reply. But she really didn't want to have an argument with her boss—or with anyone, come to that! Since her mother's death, when Mary was seven, anxiety had lodged in her heart and throat and was now a permanent resident. She felt as if she were walking a perpetual tightrope, terrified that one false move would see her fall, and there would be no net beneath to catch her.

None.

Mary didn't just work at the salon—it was also her home. Her Girl Friday position there had started out as a temporary subsidised role, but when it had ended Coral had offered her a permanent position with the added bonus of accommodation. She had also hinted at the prospect of an apprenticeship, although it had never transpired. Coral was only too happy to tell her why—aside from daydreaming, she was terrible at small talk, prone to saying the wrong thing...

Basically, she didn't fit in.

Mary had long since known that.

'This is Mary...' That was how the social workers had introduced her, often late at night, or in the middle of a family dinner. 'Mary Jones.'

Mary Jones—the 'emergency placement' that never quite worked out.

She'd been labelled 'difficult' and 'odd' by so many. Her withdrawal into grief had seen her labelled as sullen, and later attempts to be friendly had come across as desperate and clingy. Oh, how they'd laughed at one new school, when at Show and Tell she'd proudly shown the class a present her father had made her. While in prison.

Ha-ha-ha...

Now, at twenty-one, she was without a true friend, a career, or a home she could properly call her own—just a bed in the back room of the salon.

'Tonight's a chance to earn some good money,' Coral said. 'Heaven knows you moan about not having enough.'

That stung.

'I've done a lot for you,' Coral reminded her. 'Just yesterday I defended you to the other girls when the tip jar went missing.'

'That had nothing to do with me.'

'We're never going to get to the bottom of that...'

Coral sighed pointedly. 'Though it has been going missing a lot lately, and if the other girls knew about your father...' As Mary shrivelled, Coral became kinder. 'Look, if you do this for me I'll double the cash and do your hair.'

The thought of getting her hair done was actually rather tempting. Despite working in the salon, Mary had never had it professionally cut, and wore her wavy blonde hair in a low ponytail.

But still she shook her head. 'I'm sorry, no.'

Coral didn't even register her response. 'Think about it,' she said, leaving Mary standing alone in the staffroom.

She should have defended herself against the theft insinuation more strongly, Mary knew, except she always froze when her father's criminal history was raised, terrified of the deeper truth coming to light if anyone delved.

Before the petty crime he was in prison for now, there had been some white-collar crime, in his attempt to pay legal and school fees and hold on to the family home. It was the crime prior to that that Mary could not bear to revisit.

William Jones had been driving under the influence and had been charged for the death of her mother.

It was a cold summing-up, but it was all Mary could manage.

Trying to push her thoughts aside, Mary started to collect up the mugs and headed out to the little kitchenette near her bedroom. Seeing the milk had again been left out, she put it back in the fridge, but as she closed the door she paused. There, between the notes and the other quirky magnets on the door, was one precious one.

It went everywhere with Mary.

A little fridge magnet with a picture of a beach in Cornwall and a tiny little thermometer that still worked. Mary checked the temperature each morning and could almost feel her mother's smile. It had been with Mary since she had first been removed from the family home—a little gift she had bought her mother on their final family holiday.

Final everything, really.

How could she have guessed on that wonderful summer day that a few short weeks later everything would fall apart?

She ran her finger over the magnet and along the tiny thread of the thermometer, that was, despite the years, always accurate. Here, far back from the warmth of the salon, the thermometer reading was as cold as Mary was lonely.

From beneath it she pulled out a scrap of paper—a horoscope she had torn out when she'd been sorting out the salon magazines.

If today is your birthday...

Adventures awaited, apparently, if only she had the courage to take a chance...

She had torn it out partly hoping it was a sign that

her mother was showing her the path she should take. Foolish, perhaps, yet it was all the guidance she had.

As Coral called out another drink order Mary replaced the horoscope and the magnet, then made the drinks, which she took out to the clients.

'So, where are you off to tonight?' Coral was painting her nails as she chatted with a client.

Everyone was getting ready for Saturday night. Dinners, bars… Anniversaries, catching up with friends… Mary listened to the loud chatter above the hairdryers, and every now and then she could feel Coral's eyes drift to hers.

Half the clients, it seemed, were going on blind dates tonight, and surely what Coral was suggesting was much the same? The money would mean she could add to her interview outfit and bring forward her secret plans to leave.

'Have you thought any more about it?' Coral asked as the annoying bell on the door jangled when the final client left.

'I can't.'

'Eric really needs a date. Leventis will bring a knockout—you can guarantee that! Eric doesn't want to be there sitting on his own…'

Mary wavered. One of the reasons that Mary never ventured anywhere more exciting than the nearby coffee shop or the local library was that she felt conspicuous alone.

'Eric's a sweetheart,' Coral said. 'If you don't have anything to wear you can borrow a dress…'

'I have something,' Mary said, thinking of the vintage dress she had bought. It had been an impractical buy but she had been unable to resist, even though it had remained unworn.

'You're sure?' Coral checked dubiously. 'It's a very high-end hotel.'

'I have just the dress,' Mary assured her. 'I've been saving it for something special.'

'Great!' Coral beamed. 'Go and have a seat, then, and I'll sort out your hair.'

'Shouldn't it be washed first?' Mary asked, thinking of the deep conditioning treatments and the scalp massages which she saw being given each and every day.

But Coral shook her head. 'You can't wash it if you're wearing it up, and there isn't time to cut and style it. You'll have to meet him soon.'

Mary sat, watching her hair being straightened and then loosely curled at the front. She leant forward a little as Coral pinned it up and thought of her seven-year-old self in the old school report.

Reckless, mischievous, mettlesome… Except there had been another resounding theme…

Mary has to learn to consider consequences…

'Head up,' Coral said.

Mary met her own vivid blue eyes in the mirror for a second, and then closed them as Coral doused her in hairspray.

For so many years now she'd been considering consequences. Over and over until she was too scared of her own shadow to move. She was bone-weary of watching others have fun while she held herself back. So tired of being alone.

Maybe this Eric felt the same way.

'Done!' Coral said. 'I'll leave you to do your own make-up. I really have to get going. I'll see you on Tuesday.' That was when the salon opened again. 'Make sure you do the high dusting.'

'Of course,' Mary said.

'And the towels…' Coral reminded her.

The bell jangled as she dashed out the door—not that Mary was paying attention.

Tonight, on her twenty-first birthday, Mary was going on her very first date!

CHAPTER TWO

'*YOU'RE* MARY?'

Standing in the opulent lobby of the most stunning London hotel, hearing the ridicule in her date's voice, Mary knew that she had made the most dreadful mistake: Eric Ridgemont could not be described, by any stretch of the imagination, as 'a sweetheart'.

Neither was he alone—there was a trio of suited, rather burly men behind him that made Mary feel nervous also.

The greeter had already taken her coat and umbrella, or she would have been tempted to grab them back as Ridgemont's eyes ran disapprovingly down her grey tweed dress.

Plain at the front, with neat darts at the bust, it was pinched in at the waist, but the beauty was in its back—a subtle plunge that led into a long row of covered buttons that flared into a small pleated fish tail.

And it was entirely wasted on this night.

'You're late,' he reprimanded.

'My bus...' She attempted to explain but he wasn't really listening, just eyeing her up and down in a way that had Mary squirming in the pair of Coral's rather too large stilettos.

'Well, go and sort out some make-up,' he prompted, peering at her face.

'I never wear any.'

He hissed his irritation, then glanced at the time. 'We'd better go through.'

'Perhaps not.' Mary cleared her throat and, though terrified to use it, somehow found her voice. 'It's obvious that I'm not what you were expecting...'

She turned on the borrowed unfamiliar heels, rueing her mistake and preparing to face Coral's wrath, but fingers gripped her upper arm.

'Oh, no, you don't.'

As he halted her retreat Mary felt apprehension turn into white-hot fear as his fat fingers squeezed hard into sensitive flesh.

'It's far too late to do anything about it now. You'll just have to do.'

His hand slid down to her elbow and Mary was rendered mute for a moment as they were led through the reception area and into a restaurant.

Under any other circumstances she would have stood a moment, simply to take it all in, for it was more beautiful than any place she had ever been. There were chandeliers laden with gorgeous crystals that danced light around the room, and Mary felt certain that this had once been or was even still used as a ballroom. But while the hotel was tasteful and sublime, the company was not.

'Did Coral tell you who we're dining with?' Eric checked once they'd been seated.

'Briefly.' Mary nodded, though she was too nervous to recall the name. 'I'm sorry, I've forgotten.'

'Leventis.' He saw her nonplussed expression. 'Costa Leventis. He has a lot of property across Europe, though you're probably more interested in the gossip sites. He frequently appears there...'

Mary blinked, a whisper of an image returning to her from the cover of a magazine. 'Some scandal on a yacht...?' she said, as she tried to recall. 'Or in a casino...?'

'There's scandal wherever Leventis goes—though he's gone to ground lately. He's an arrogant bastard. New money...' Eric sniffed. 'Needs the occasional reminder about who gave him his start. No doubt he'll have some siren with him. Just entertain her while I find out what the hell he's up to.'

He leant in closer and gave Mary a look that made her shudder inwardly.

'There might be a bonus in it for you tonight.'

She felt a trickle of sweat between her breasts and, despite the opulence of her surroundings, in that moment she would have given anything to be back at the small bedsit in the rear of the hair salon.

Oh, whatever have I let myself be talked into?

Mary desperately wanted out. 'I only agreed to dinner,' Mary said, determined to state it upfront.

But this man wasn't listening. 'The night ends when I tell you and not a moment before. Let's not forget that you're being paid very well. So right here, right now, I'm telling you to lose the attitude and damn well smile.'

It would be far too obvious if she were to get up and leave now, Mary decided, but in a few moments she would excuse herself and head to the restrooms. Then she would get the hell away.

Except the three men who had accompanied Eric were seated at the next table!

She suddenly remembered her old ballet teacher ordering her to smile, and somehow she did just that, while still planning her escape.

'That's better,' he said. 'And remember…'

His voice halted mid-sentence as the mood in the room suddenly changed, everybody's attention suddenly diverted. Not just Eric's and not just Mary's. The whole room turned—even waiters stopped for a brief second. Everybody was looking at the man who was entering the restaurant.

Costa Leventis was *not* what she was expecting.

Nor was her reaction.

Inexplicably she shivered, for it felt as if she'd just recognised a friend.

And Mary had no friends.

He was tall. Not just tall, but noticeably so. With black, longish wavy hair, he was distinctly unshaven. Given it was black-tie only, and he was not wearing one, a critic might say he was disrespecting the room. But as he approached she watched the fluid lines of his immaculately cut black suit which he wore with a black shirt. He was without a doubt the most naturally elegant person in the room.

She'd expected from Eric's brief description someone brasher, and certainly younger, but she guessed he was in his mid-thirties. It would seem there was no one with him for Mary to 'entertain', for he had entered the restaurant alone.

Given the distasteful company she found herself keeping, Mary wasn't quite sure why the sight of such an imposing man should feel something of a relief. Yet it did.

Safety in numbers, Mary told herself as she pushed her shaking legs to a stand on his approach.

'Eric.' Costa Leventis nodded as he shook Eric's outstretched hand and then turned to Mary, briefly acknowledging her. 'This is…?' he politely enquired, holding out his hand.

There was a bit of hesitation from Eric as he searched his short-term memory. 'Mary.'

'Mary?' he repeated, perhaps expecting a fuller introduction.

'Mary from London,' she replied as he took her hand and briefly shook it.

'An unusual surname.'

She frowned, at first a little bemused by his words, then kicked herself for her stupid response.

But there was no time to rectify it. And this man clearly did not need her surname, for his attention had already moved back to Eric, and it would seem Costa had a question for him.

'We were supposed to be meeting at the bar, and yet they told me you were waiting for me in here?'

'Of course.' Eric nodded. 'It's your first night back in London and it's been far too long since we sat down to dinner.'

'Is that so?' Costa said as they took their seats.

He looked as if he was the kind of man loathed anyone making presumptive claims on his time, and Ridgemont was speaking like a disgruntled lover.

'How long are you here for?' Ridgemont asked.

'It depends,' Costa responded evasively. He turned to the hovering waiter and ordered his favourite cognac.

'I was thinking champagne rather than brandy.'

Eric gave a short burst of laughter and Mary realised that in Costa's presence he was actually nervous.

'There's a lot to celebrate after all.'

'Champagne for Mr Ridgemont,' Costa said, and then glanced over to her. 'Mary?'

She shook her head. 'I'm fine.'

'Have some champagne,' Eric pushed.

'No, thank you,' she insisted, her anxiety rising, because surely if he were her real date then Eric would know that she didn't drink. But oughtn't she to join in if there was to be a celebratory toast? 'I'll have sparkling water, please.'

'Champagne for the table,' Eric snapped to the patient waiter.

But Costa simply overrode the order, as if he had not even heard Eric's terse demand. 'Cognac, sparkling water, and champagne for Mr Ridgemont.'

'Of course, sir. Would you like menus?'

'Just the drinks,' Costa said, and then added, 'thank you.'

No champagne for Costa, no menus… Even to Mary's inexperienced eyes it was obvious that the dinner Eric had engineered was not going as planned.

Costa was in complete command, and possibly the only unperturbed person in the restaurant!

Every woman in the room, Mary was certain, was distinctly on edge and casting little glances in the direction of their table—or rather in the direction of Costa. Even all the men had paused and glanced over when he'd entered, with something Mary could only liken to respect or admiration.

He was company that many would like to keep, Mary concluded, whether personally or professionally. Yet the empty seat beside him spoke volumes—Costa was not here to impress anyone. And that empty seat spoke of restlessness too. It said that this was only a small part of his plans for the night.

His gaze briefly roamed the restaurant and Mary was certain that all he'd have to do was meet the eyes of one of the many women he held entranced and she would simply get up and walk over to be seated beside him.

Mary would rather like to do the same!

There was an energy to him that was compelling. Even his voice had captured her thought processes—it was low and deep, and though heavily laced with a rich accent his English was near perfect as he addressed Eric.

'I had reserved a quiet spot at the bar so that we could speak undisturbed and in private.'

'There's nothing that can't be said here.' Eric dismissed Costa's concerns. 'Mary knows we'll be talking business, don't you, darling…?'

He reached and took her hand, but as he moved to plant his wet mouth on her cheek Mary couldn't help but flinch, darting her head to the side in an attempt to avoid his touch.

But there was no escaping the wetness of his lips on her cheek.

It was her first kiss since childhood.

And it was a form of contact that Mary had thought she craved.

Yet she sat there, feeling utterly revolted, and as Eric spoke on she surreptitiously reached for her napkin and dabbed her cheek.

'Costa and I go way back,' Eric said to Mary—though not for her benefit, she was sure. 'How long have you been in business now, Costa…? Fifteen years?'

'Oh, I'd say it was longer.'

'It can't be.' Eric shook his head. 'You were just twenty when I backed that loan for the Anapliró resort?'

'Retreat,' Costa corrected.

'And you're how old now?'

'Thirty-five.'

'There you go, then.' Eric was triumphant. 'I knew I was right.'

Mary glanced over, and Costa's brief, almost imperceptible smile told her that Eric only thought he had won and had in fact just been duped. Gosh, there was something far more than champagne and business going on at this table, and if she hadn't been so petrified then Mary would have been riveted.

It was then that Costa looked over to her and she properly met his eyes.

His expression was completely unreadable, though it could never be described as blank, for there was far too much knowing in his eyes. She could not, even on close inspection, define their colour—a mix of silver, black and grey, as if angels had crushed onyx and diamonds and at the last moment thrown a chip of emerald into the mortar. And they had ground in some sapphire with their pestle too, for, yes, there was a glimmer of blue…

Had she not been sitting beside the most appalling man imaginable, there might have been a moment for her to consider that Costa was truly beautiful. Except as Eric spoke Costa flicked his gaze away, and Mary saw his flash of contempt for the man who sat opposite him. She sensed danger.

'A right slag heap, wasn't it?' Eric continued, and without turning his head he addressed Mary again. 'Costa grew up there.'

'Did you?' Mary politely enquired, and Costa gave a brief nod.

'Not that he told me so at the time.'

'I wouldn't have merited your attention if I had,' Costa said, and unlike Eric he did not use Mary as a channel to deliver his words.

Eric continued to do so, though. 'I have to hand it to him,' he droned, 'Costa saw its potential. God knows how, though. Still, without my backing...' He carried on, puffing himself up at every turn. And while he seemed to be speaking to Mary, it was all an attempt to belittle Costa.

And it was a futile attempt, Mary knew, because Costa Leventis remained utterly composed.

'Well, it's history now...' Eric said. 'To be honest, I'm glad to be shot of the last piece of it.' He looked around. 'Where the hell are our drinks? I want to toast our foray into the Middle East. Ah, here they are...'

Costa had been looking forward to this moment for what felt like a lifetime—in fact he had been planning it for most of his own. Yes, this went back way past fifteen years.

He thought of his very first purchase: a single room in a seedy hotel. At the time, Anapliró's only one. It had been far from an impulse buy. And what he'd told Eric was right. Eric would never have exchanged so much as a glance with a poor boy from Anapliró, nor a desperate woman collapsed on the floor, come to that. Oh, there were many reasons for him to relish this moment to come.

But as he went to deliver his well-rehearsed spiel he glanced over to Ridgemont's date and knew, simply knew, that Eric's vile temper would find an outlet. That this 'Mary from London' would bear the brunt of Costa's actions this night.

Whatever her relationship with Ridgemont, it should not affect this business meeting.

Ridgemont's choice of date for the night and the consequences to her of the news he was about to impart would not usually enter his head.

Costa was not an unkind person. It was more that he had trained himself to be an unemotional one.

Except…

His gaze flicked to her, and then away, although with that brief glance the details he had taken in were stamped on his mind. She wore a very simple grey dress and no make-up or jewellery. Her blonde hair was styled and pinned up—all that he knew. But it was not her delicate bone structure, nor the sapphire of her blue eyes that played on his mind. It was more that there was a certain prudence to her that disquieted his soul.

There was a certain naivety too, which did not quite equate—for he was beyond certain that Ridgemont would have paid for her company. She troubled him, and Costa wanted to be the hell away from trouble—hence this meeting tonight.

She was like a little bird, sitting on a ledge, alert and nervous but with no real idea of the might of the tigers that prowled beneath.

Oh, despite Galen's warning, Costa doubted there would be a scene. Costa would deliver his news, and Eric would posture, but then he'd bluster off with his posse in tow. Then there would be perhaps a week of difficult meetings, followed by the legal fallout, for which Costa had been long prepared. But now there was an unexpected issue that had arisen—one he had not considered at all when he'd carefully made his plans: the fact that Ridgemont would storm off into the night with *her*.

'Cheers,' Ridgemont said, and held up his glass. 'What is it they say in Greece? *Yamas!*'

'*Yamas,*' Costa duly answered, and decided he would drink to improving Ridgemont's black soul. 'To your health…'

He clinked Ridgemont's glass and then looked over to Mary. How the hell did he clink her glass and wish her well when he knew she would be leaving with that pig?

Costa felt something that he didn't even want

to acknowledge…something that verged on protectiveness for a woman to whom he had barely spoken.

Costa Leventis did not clink her glass—not that Eric noticed—and Mary sat, wishing the ground would open up and she might simply disappear. Except she felt safe at the moment. Relieved by Costa's presence. Which was odd, for it was clear that everyone else seemed set on edge by him. Eric was now sweating with nerves, and the waiters were all waiting to pounce, and still so many heads turned towards him.

'So!' With the formalities over, Eric pushed for answers. 'I'm assuming there's a reason for your early arrival?'

'Indeed…'

There was a certain ominous note to Costa's tone that forced attention, and as the waiter approached again to offer menus, or another drink perhaps, Costa waved him away with a perfectly manicured hand.

He was going to leave, Mary realised, and she suddenly dreaded what he was about to say.

And that she would be left with this man.

'I didn't want to put it in an email or talk through a screen…' Costa knew his voice was calm, eerily so. 'You know I prefer to speak face to face.'

'We can't wait to hear—can we, darling?' Ridgemont said.

Costa watched as he again reached for Mary's pale hand and squeezed it. The tips of her slender fingers turned a bloodless white, and very deliberately Costa did not blink. Glancing up from her hand, he registered fear in her eyes.

Costa's gaze flicked back to Ridgemont. 'I would rather speak with you alone.'

'Of course.' Mary, flustered, took her cue... 'Please excuse me for a moment.'

Eric was still gripping her hand, but as she stood he had no choice but to release it. She put down her napkin and made a rushed excuse about finding the powder room.

She walked briskly away, asking a waiter to direct her, but then she turned and looked back at the table. Mentally kicking herself, she realised she had left her purse there.

Costa saw that she had too. He saw the tatty evening bag with its fraying handle and then he glanced over to where she was making her way through the restaurant. Her gait told him she was struggling in heels that didn't fit properly. He saw her look back, and in that very second she again met his gaze. He was certain then that she'd been looking for an opportunity to flee.

It was only for a second, perhaps less, that their eyes met, and Mary did not quite understand the almost imperceptible nod he gave. Was he thanking her for leaving them alone, perhaps? Telling her to take her time before coming back maybe?

She truly didn't know.

Blindly she turned and pushed open the door to the powder room and stood gripping the sink, trying and failing to calm down as she worked out what she should do.

Good news was not being delivered out there, Mary was certain. She would not be returning to smiles and celebrations!

Though she knew she should just get the hell out, her purse held the salon keys, and the little money she had, as well as her travel card, and this smart hotel was an awfully long way from home.

Home.

She let out a mirthless laugh that was more a strangled sob, for though she had been lonely for a very long time, never had Mary felt quite so alone.

Tonight—on her birthday—it was especially hard to accept that she had no one to call on to ask for help. Really, there was not a single soul who would notice if she didn't make it home tonight.

A missing person…unmissed.

Mary pressed her fingers into her eyes. Almost fourteen years after her mother's death, she still missed her each and every day.

She still spoke to her. In her head, of course. But for Mary, all motherly advice had run out at the age of seven, and there was nothing she could draw on for nights such as these.

Except…

She heard the once steady voice of her father: *'You go up to someone and ask for help…'*

She could remember her daddy telling her what to do if she got lost in a shop or parted from her group on a field trip or such.

'A police officer if you can see one, or a woman…'

Mary peeled her hands from her face, feeling calmer now, knowing what she could do. She would head out to Reception and there ask them to retrieve her bag for her and that they see her into a taxi. She couldn't afford one, of course, but she had her emergency funds. And if Coral fired her, well…

Mary had already decided she was leaving her job anyway.

Oh, she'd prefer to have a new job lined up, as well as some accommodation, but those issues rather paled into insignificance right now.

Braver now, but still terrified, she smoothed down her dress and then popped a loose curl behind her ear. She took a deep, calming breath before heading out, her intention to exit the restaurant.

Except a brief glance at the table revealed only Costa sitting there, drumming his fingers. Furthermore, Eric Ridgemont's men were nowhere to be seen, so Mary decided to retrieve her purse herself.

And then leave.

On closer inspection, Costa Leventis looked irritated.

Decidedly so.

Costa was way more than irritated—all his plans had been blown out of the water, for when it had come down to it he hadn't told Ridgemont he was severing all ties. Instead Costa had sent him off to an exclusive party and said he would join him there soon.

Why?

It was a good question, and one he was having trouble accepting the answer to.

His whole night had been upended all because of this 'Mary from London', who meant precisely nothing to him.

Costa glanced up as she made her way back. He did not stand as she approached. In fact, it was only when she reached for her purse that he spoke. 'He's gone.'

Mary assumed he meant that Eric had gone to the restroom and that his security men had accompanied him. Of course she did not tell Costa of her plan to flee. Instead, she quickly came up with a reason to be reaching for her purse, even if she had no make-up either on her face or in it!

'I forgot my lipstick.'

'Mary,' he said, in a rather world-weary voice

that had her looking over at him. 'Ridgemont hasn't just gone to the restroom—he has left for the night.'

And it would seem that Costa Leventis was doing the same, for he was standing now.

Goodness, he really was tall.

Mary was five foot two, plus her borrowed six-inch heels, yet he still stood head and shoulders above her.

'Is he waiting for me...?' she asked, her eyes glancing to the exit, envisaging Ridgemont pacing in the lobby waiting for her and, even worse, angry, especially if he and Costa had just had a row.

'No, I told him about a party taking place in Soho—it's invitation-only. I'm supposed to be joining him there later.'

'Oh.'

'It's not the sort of party where one generally arrives with a date.'

Double oh!

Thank goodness!

She had no idea what had just occurred and she wasn't sure she ever wanted to find out. Still, it was obvious the night was over—and she was clearly the worst escort in the world, for she hadn't even been paid. The thought came as a relief—her regretful brief foray into this world was officially over and done with.

She had walked into the restaurant with Ridgemont and was walking out with Costa, but her legs were shaky, for she was still unsure as to what had happened in between.

Actually, she felt a little ill.

'I'll say goodnight,' Costa said, and moved to head off and return to the quiet table he had reserved at the bar before Ridgemont had attempted to railroad him.

Except then Costa was suddenly cross, and turned and faced her. 'I'm going to tell you something, "Mary from London".' He pointed one of his beautifully manicured fingers at hers. 'Don't mess with the big guns. Don't play games when you don't know the rules.'

'I have no idea what you're talking about,' she attempted. 'And actually my name is Mary Jones.'

'I don't need your name,' Costa said, but for clarity's sake put things more bluntly. 'Just know this— I saved your ass tonight.'

CHAPTER THREE

'EXCUSE ME!' MARY blustered at his crude words.

But Costa was non-repentant and he repeated himself. 'I just saved your ass.'

'Look, I'm not sure what you're referring to,' she attempted, trying to spare herself the shame of being outed as a paid-for date. 'If things were a bit strained earlier then it was because Eric and I were both a bit flustered—I was late... I missed my bus...'

Her voice trailed off at his slight eyebrow raise. Possibly, Mary realised, if she were really in a relationship with Eric they would have arrived together—and certainly not via public transport.

And so, in a vague, misplaced stab at redemption, she used Coral's description of him. 'He's a sweetheart.'

'Really?' An incredulous smile spread on Costa's lips. 'Then I apologise for the misunderstanding. I told Ridgemont the party invitation was strictly for one.' He had long since refused to be on first name terms with that man. 'But I can easily let him know I've added you to the guest list if you want to join him…'

He watched dull colour spread from her neck to her cheeks, but there was dignity in her reply.

'That won't be necessary.'

She looked embarrassed at being caught out, but he also saw her sudden flood of relief that this nightmare really was over.

'I should leave,' Mary said, sounding flustered. And she turned to do just that.

He let her go with a brief nod.

In fact, now that the so-called 'meeting' was over, Costa took his phone from his jacket pocket and turned it on. While waiting for it to load, he glanced up. Previously he had noticed only her nerves and her ill-fitting shoes. Now, though, he saw that her dress was not so plain. The slight dip at the back allowed a glimpse of pale spine and accentuated her tiny waist.

There was an old-fashioned beauty to her, Costa thought, as she nervously tiptoed through Reception on little matchstick legs. There was something about this Mary Jones that forced his attention.

He turned back to his phone and tried to swat her from his mind, but found himself looking up again. She hadn't got very far—in fact she stood nearby at a table. The flush from her face had gone and she was suddenly incredibly pale as she dragged in air and looked around nervously, as if in dread that Ridgemont might suddenly appear.

'Mary.' To his own surprise Costa walked over. 'Are you all right?'

'Fine,' she attempted.

But she was suddenly overwhelmed by her own foolishness, recalling her trembling fear as she had practically hidden in the restroom, planning her escape.

'Well, not fine, exactly. I've had better Saturday nights…'

She let out a shrill laugh, because actually she'd had nothing but a string of miserable Saturday nights, but right now she'd settle for an evening spent folding a mountain of pink towels back at the salon, slowly losing more of her spirit.

'I just need a moment.'

'You're okay,' Costa said, even though she looked as if she might faint.

He had already noticed her very slender frame and he felt a sudden twist of guilt—for they had missed dinner, after all, and perhaps she had been counting on it. Costa knew better than most the true pain of hunger and how it felt to be denied a much-needed meal.

'Would you like to get something to eat?' Costa

offered. 'Perhaps catch your breath before you head off?'

'No, thank you.'

'We could go into the bar…'

'You warned me yourself not to mess with the big guns,' Mary responded rather tartly, when usually she'd never dare. But adrenaline was still coursing through her veins. 'And I'm guessing—' from Eric's nerves, from the deference of the waiter, she'd realised that perhaps this Costa was the one to fear '—I'm guessing you are one.'

'Unlike Ridgemont, I don't pay for company,' Costa responded. 'Now, you can take that as an insult and huff off, or we can take a seat here and at least get a drink…'

He gestured to the sumptuous bar with its occasional tables and carefully placed leather chairs and velvet couches, as well as an open fire. Despite its size, and the people filling the seats, it reminded her of a cosy nook. A place to simply curl up and hide.

'It is up to you.'

She looked to the brass doors she had first walked through. A second ago all she had wanted was to get the hell away, but she could see the arriving patrons with their umbrellas, could see the black of the night outside, and suddenly she felt safer with him than alone.

'*Just* a drink?'

'Yes, Mary, I don't do double-speak.'

'Meaning…?'

'If I wanted sex I would say so upfront.'

She let out another burst of nervous laughter, but he did not join her. Instead, he repeated his offer.

'Would you like to join me for a drink before you leave?'

Finally she could breathe. For the first time since arriving in the hotel she felt air expand right down to the bottom of her lungs. Yes, a drink sounded like something she would very much like, if only to gather herself.

'Please.'

They were led through to where gorgeous couples and groups were sipping their beverages and making conversation. Again, she noticed that certain pause as they passed.

He had an effect on everyone, Mary realised, but then she wondered if all these people were simply curious as to what on earth he was doing with a woman in someone else's shoes carrying a rather scruffy purse.

The bar area was sophisticated indeed, and his reserved table was tucked away in a gorgeous alcove, with plump chesterfield chairs and a low walnut table. There was a violet orchid floating in a small glass jar, but there was no candle or anything to denote romance—this was where, she realised, he had been intending to speak with Eric.

Thank God he had gone.

Gratefully she sank into a seat as he did the same, and for a moment closed her eyes in quiet relief. Cos-

ta's rather indelicate dressing-down had hit home. Indeed, had he not intervened, Mary knew she might
well have found herself in serious trouble tonight.

'Shall I ask for the menu?' Costa broke into her
thoughts. 'I wouldn't mind something to eat.'

'Go ahead,' she said. 'I'll just have…' She looked
up to the waiter. 'A hot chocolate, please.'

'That's not some cocktail I don't know about, is
it?' Costa checked, and for the first time she properly smiled. Not a big smile, a subtle one, but unlike before it wasn't forced.

'No, just a hot chocolate.'

'With marshmallows?' the waiter checked.

'Yes, please!' It was so nice to be asked that she
dared ask for more. 'Extra-sweet, please.'

'Of course.'

Costa gave his own drink order and ordered
some nibbles, then they made polite small talk as
they waited for them to arrive—or rather, Mary
tried to. She was truly awful at it, though.

'The weather is dreadful,' she said.

'It always is when I come to London.'

'I don't think that's very fair.'

Costa shrugged. 'It's just an observation, not an
insult—I've never had a sunny day here.'

'Well…it was gorgeous yesterday.' Why was she
defending the weather? Mary had no idea.

'That was yesterday. I can assure you there will
be solid rain all week.'

'Is that how long you're in London, then?'

'Yes,' Costa said, a touch surprised that he had given this information away so readily, for he usually kept his plans to himself.

Always.

'I'll keep an umbrella handy, then,' Mary said.

'Do.'

Then there was no more small talk. Mary just sat, somewhat defeated, and Costa simply let her be.

Their drinks were served—his preferred cognac and for Mary hot chocolate in a delicate porcelain cup and saucer, along with some delectable tiny pastries and chocolate-dipped fruits.

'This is lovely,' she said, having taken a sip of the velvety drink and seemingly revelled in its sweet warmth.

'Enjoy,' Costa said, surprised at his relief when she picked up the tongs and selected some food.

Despite his determination not to get involved, he knew he could not leave the sum total of their conversation as a discussion of the weather.

'So,' Costa prompted, 'tell me about you…'

It sounded like a clichéd opening, except it was a line he had never used before. But she really intrigued him and he found he couldn't help himself.

'There's really not much to tell.'

'I doubt that.'

'I work at a hairdresser's.'

She told him the name of it And he shook his head. It was probably the kind of place a man like him would never set foot in.

'Do you like it?' he asked.

'Some days.'

She popped a little ball of chocolate-dipped pastry into her mouth. Costa wondered whether it was to stop him from delving further, but he knew delaying tactics and waited till she had swallowed.

'And are your family in London too?' he enquired, before she could reach for more food.

'I have no family,' Mary said, and even as she lied she looked him right in the eye.

It was, in truth, a practised lie.

A necessary lie.

But that didn't stop her feeling guilty each time she said it.

It had meant survival at school, and that had been confirmed when her boss, Coral, had warned her not to reveal that her father was in prison, so her response had become the norm. Anyway, this man did not need to know; he was making conversation, that was all.

'None?' Costa checked.

'None,' Mary said firmly, and took another sip of her drink. But she herself heard the slight rattle as she replaced the cup in its saucer.

Costa had noted it too, though his eyes did not move to her hands. Instead he watched the blink of her gorgeous blue eyes and she knew he didn't believe her.

'Is it hard being alone in the world?' he asked.

Then, as if taken aback by his own curiosity, immediately apologised. 'Excuse me. I had no right to ask that.'

'It's fine.' In fact, it was refreshing to be asked. 'I guess I'm used to it, for the most part.'

'What about the other parts?'

'Other parts?'

She was about to offer a tight smile and reach for a white chocolate ball, except there was a gentleness to his questioning and he no longer seemed imposing, simply kind. He was patient too, for they sat in a gentle silence as she actually thought about those 'other parts'. Yes, she had lied about not having a father, but this man in front of her had no right to the secrets of her heart.

And so she thought not so much about the emptiness of Christmas, nor the desperation of the unmarked birthday that had led her here tonight. No, Mary thought of the hollow ache of loneliness. The moments when she woke up in fright over a problem to be faced alone. How she had felt just a short while ago in the restroom as if she could simply disappear from the face of the earth unnoticed...

He watched her eyes finally lift to his. 'I feel somewhat adrift.'

'Adrift?'

'It means—'

'I know what it means,' Costa said, for it was not the English he was having trouble comprehending.

'Still…' She gave him a smile then. 'It means that I get to make my own choices…'

'What were you doing with Ridgemont?' he asked, and watched her rapid blink in response. 'I have known him for many years and I've never once heard him described as a sweetheart—even I didn't want to be here tonight.'

'Then why were you?' Mary asked.

'Touché.' He gave a grim smile. 'You don't really expect me to answer that, do you?'

'No…' Mary admitted, but she did make an observation. 'Though from the vibe at the table I could sense you weren't about to deliver pleasant news.'

Costa said nothing.

'You've known him longer than fifteen years, haven't you?'

He shot her a look, not really surprised by her perceptiveness, more that she was bold enough to ask.

And Costa liked boldness.

'I have known him for longer.'

Usually Costa would not have given even that much away, let alone elaborate, but he had been primed for things to come to an abrupt end tonight and been denied the satisfaction of the moment. Despite his cool demeanour, he was still riled.

'Ridgemont wouldn't recall, though. He had his team of minders with him even back then.'

'Really?'

Costa refused to be drawn further. 'Look, forgive me if I sound presumptuous… I don't tend to concern myself with someone else's date, but that's because I generally know they can take care of themselves. You, though, seemed out of your depth. More than that, you seemed to realise that for yourself.'

Mary was silent.

'Am I right?'

She could lie no more when the truth was blatantly clear. Had she not forgotten her bag in her dash to the powder room she would now be sitting in a taxi she couldn't afford and almost home.

'Yes.' She looked right at him then. 'My boss assured me—'

'Your *boss* needs to vet your clients better,' Costa said sharply.

Oh, God, he thought she was referring to her *madam*, or whatever they were called! But there was more on her mind than enlightening him…

'Might he come back?' she asked. 'When he finds out the party isn't real.'

'It's real,' Costa said. 'Though I doubt they'll be thrilled by his arrival. You're correct, our meeting was not going to be a pleasant one, but instead of telling him what I came to say, I called in a favour to get him away from you.'

Oh!

'I was about to make a run for it…' she admitted. 'Look, I made a mistake—'

She stopped. He didn't need to know about the pressure applied by Coral that had brought her here this evening, but there was also the real reason she'd finally succumbed tonight, and something about Costa Leventis made her feel safe enough to reveal it.

'I just wanted a fabulous night out…somewhere nice.'

'There *are* safer ways to chase excitement, Mary.'

And he would know all of them, Mary thought. She stifled an involuntary sigh. There was a shot of silver at his temples, a little fan of lines beside those gorgeous eyes… He just oozed worldliness and experience and…and something else. Something she was struggling to place. He had a kind of 'knowing' about him, and she felt so drab and unsophisticated in comparison.

'So,' he said, holding the stem of his glass between two fingers, swirling it slowly as he warmed it with his palm before taking a taste of cognac, 'how old are you?'

'Twenty-one,' Mary said and then sighed. 'Today.'

He said nothing to that. In fact he looked distinctly unimpressed. Not, of course, that she'd expected him to break into song, but she seemed destined to tick off another birthday entirely un-acknowledged.

He fired another question. 'How long have you been working...' he hesitated '...at the hairdresser's?'

'Almost five years.'

'Years?' Costa checked.

'Yes,' Mary said. 'I started there when I was six-teen. It's not ideal, of course.'

'Is that why you're here on a Saturday night? Trying to earn some extra cash?'

She said nothing. In fact, she was trying to hold back from devouring the plate of nibbles and try-ing to remember her manners, given that he had so far not touched the food.

Costa wasn't holding back on the questions though. 'I assume you are paid in cash?'

'I don't think that's a polite question.'

Costa took a breath and knew not to push it, but he loathed more than anything people being taken advantage of, and God knew he'd been on the re-ceiving end often enough while trying to get ahead.

'Could you get another job?' he asked, despite his determination to endure only a quick drink with her and then walk away. 'One that pays you enough to pay your rent *and* eat?'

She pulled her hand back from the rapidly dimin-ishing food selection. But instead of shrivelling, as she usually did, she shot him a look. 'Why do you think I'm here, Costa?'

'I get it, okay?' He did—and what was more, he admired her. 'I know it's easier said than done. Go ahead…' he said, and pushed the platter towards her. 'They are not to my taste.'

'Then why did you order them?'

'I get a little mixed up at times. I thought I had asked for *orekita*…' He saw her frown. *'Meze.'* Still the frown.

In truth, Costa knew exactly what he had ordered, but he had noted her sweet drink choice and taken a guess that she would enjoy it.

'In Greece the selection would be more savoury.'

'Well, this is perfect for me.'

'Then enjoy. I shall have something else later. You were saying you don't like where you work…? That it is less than ideal?' Costa prompted.

She gave a mirthless laugh. *'So* far from ideal. I was promised an apprenticeship when I started, but I'm not very good with the clients. I tend to say the wrong thing.'

'Say nothing,' he suggested. 'I can't stand getting my hair cut. Hairdressers always speak…' He made a yapping gesture. 'Maybe you should open a salon that offers a haircut with no conversation? Men would come in droves…'

Mary smiled. 'Well, whatever the case, it's not easy to leave without references—' She stopped herself.

'And without the right clothes for an interview at a high-end salon?' Costa suggested, but her lips tightened and he knew she felt criticised. 'May I say you look very beautiful tonight…?' He could have said so much more than that. He *wanted* to say so much more than that. But he chose not to. 'Your dress is stunning.'

He tried not make it sound sleazy or practised, to put a kindness in his tone. It was clearly so unfamiliar to her it made her blink.

Costa saw that blink as if in slow motion—the golden honey colour of her thick eyelashes as they closed—and although his faith had never lapsed, tonight it was proved…for it would seem that mountains did indeed move.

The entire reason he was sitting here was the simple fact that she moved him.

Outside family, which consisted only of his mother, he could count on one hand the people who moved him—or rather on one finger… Or make that no one. No one really moved Costa Leventis—he had trained himself in that long, long ago.

'Does your phone always buzz like that?' Mary asked, for it was lit up like a Christmas tree and sliding across the smooth walnut table with a life of its own.

He glanced at the phone. 'Excuse me for a moment.' He stood and took the call as he walked off. 'Hey, Roula.'

With his back to her, she was finally able to properly stare. He signalled to a waiter, she presumed to get the bill, then returned to his call as she unashamedly took in the exquisite cut of his suit—or rather the sheer exquisiteness of *him*.

Her first assessment had been right—he was exceptionally tall—but it wasn't just his height that held her attention. Nor the heady scent of his cologne that had stirred the air as he moved away and lingered even now…

Mary was befuddled. She told herself it was his presence, his being, his quiet command that had brought to this wretched night a sense of calmness and safety.

She turned her attention to the pretty flower on their table as Costa ended the call and returned to his seat.

Costa still couldn't quite articulate why he was prolonging the night, but there was something about her plight that moved him. Something about Mary in her old-fashioned dress that made him want to… well, to help. And fortunately he was in a position to do so.

'Sorry about that,' he said as he re-took his seat. 'I don't often take calls mid-conversation. Usually I turn my phone off…'

He did so now, for it was something that had always irritated Costa. When he gave his attention he gave it fully. However, the call had been an important one, and he had followed it up with one of his own.

'That's fine.'

'I wanted to confirm something before I put it to you.' He looked over at her. 'I have a business proposal…'

Oh, God. She really had jumped out of the frying pan and into the fire, Mary thought. The panic that had subsided over their drinks rushed back with a vengeance.

'I don't think so.'

She reached for her purse, but before she could stand he clarified his words.

'I meant a traineeship at one of my hotels. Although I don't have any here in the UK…'

'You mean an actual job?'

'Yes. You heard me discussing the retreat in Anapliró? Despite Ridgemont's description, it's actually very beautiful. We don't generally take trainees at the spa there, but we can always make room for good staff.'

Her eyes narrowed. 'In the massage parlour?'

'Can we please move away from that?' he suggested, but acknowledged her caution. 'The spa is world-renowned…more than accredited…' He lingered on the topic for a second more, as if to make one thing very clear. 'Despite the nature of our meeting, let me assure you that there is no ulterior motive. I'm barely there…'

'Why not?'

Now it was Costa who blinked. 'Excuse me?'

'If it's so beautiful, and if it's your home, then why are you barely there?'

He should tell her this minute why she wasn't successful in applying for jobs: Mary Jones really did not interview well!

There were places in an interview, especially with Costa, that people just did not go!

'That's irrelevant,' he told her. 'Is it something you would like to consider?'

Mary dared not consider it.

She dared not think about it for she wanted to leap to Anapliró in one single bound.

But even if she still didn't know how to start unpacking her feelings towards her father, Mary knew she could not abandon him.

She simply couldn't.

Costa watched her silently wrestle. What was stopping her? he pondered. Yes, he was perhaps being arrogant to assume she would simply torch her life here, but an offer of a traineeship at his retreat was so coveted there was more chance of milk from a bull. More to the point, here she was dealing with the likes of Ridgemont, for God's sake...

Perhaps that was it.

'Mary, if you have a criminal record, just tell me now and—'

'I do not!' Mary bristled.

'Fine, then.' He glanced over to the waiter and signalled him. 'Mary?' He was still waiting for an answer, which was something Costa was rather unused to in *all* walks of life. 'Would you like my staff to contact you?'

'That won't be necessary.'

She never cried—not since the night of her mother's funeral—and she certainly wouldn't start now. But she could almost taste the salt of the tears she would shed later as she declined this opportunity.

'Thank you, but no.'

'I'm very sorry to hear that.'

Not as sorry as she!

Mary shot him a look then—a sharp look, an angry look…one Mary herself didn't understand. For it was aimed at the one person who had thrown her a lifeline.

It was the most honest she had ever been with her eyes, because it was hurting her so much to decline. Her mask did not just slip—it was *gone*, and for a moment she was lost in his silvery eyes.

He did not judge.

Nor did he move to persuade or dissuade her.

He was done with her.

And then there came a moment so rare and so scarce that Mary didn't know what it was—she saw him simply accept her silent anger. Her regret.

And not just regret for declining a dream job.

There was regret yet to come, because her refusal surely meant the end of this moment.

This moment with him.

It was as if the lights had been turned off and all noise had been muted. As if the lens through which she had until now viewed the world had sharpened its focus.

All the details she had gathered through the night seemed to *click, click, click…* Not just the beauty of his eyes, but the silver at his temples, his scent, his height, his arrogance combined with such kindness… All of it clicked into one vivid image and there he was, as if for the first time.

Costa Leventis.

Yes, he was gorgeous.

Yes, he was the most attractive man she'd ever seen in real life.

But all of that she had known on sight.

She hadn't, until now, known that this man might arouse in her a reaction she had never so much as imagined—hadn't known that for all the trouble she had simultaneously ignored and anticipated tonight, this might be the most perplexing part.

It wasn't that she fancied him—that was a horrible word, and so inadequate to describe this moment when she felt as if the only other person in the world was seated in front of her.

And this moment suddenly terrified her half to death.

'I have to go.'

'Mary—' He moved to halt her.

'Do you run around offering work to all of Eric's dates?' Of course he didn't. 'Thank you for the drink…' Mary said, gathering her purse as she stood, desperate to flee.

'Please wait a moment.'

'For what?' Mary snapped, for she did not want him to glimpse what was happening inside her. She was blushing and stumbling, and hungry for cold air. 'I really do have to go.'

'Wait, please,' Costa said. 'There was another reason I interrupted our conversation…'

He glanced across the room and, perplexed, she followed his gaze. That lens widened again, and the rest of the world reappeared in slow motion… Only now she stood on what she could only describe as an entirely different plane of existence.

A waiter was walking towards them, and at that second the pianist started to play 'Happy Birthday' and everyone in the plush bar turned to stare… Mary blushed, lit up with desire, and it felt to her that every single person in the bar who was now staring at her could surely see it.

Mutely, she sat down as a perfect slice of strawberry Fraisier cake with a candle on the top was placed in front of her. Written on the plate in chocolate was *Happy 21st Birthday, Mary.*

She had lost the ability to speak.

'I think you're supposed to blow out the candle,' said Costa.

'Oh, yes…' She took a breath.

'Make a wish,' he reminded her.

She nodded. Her wish was suddenly an urgent one: *Please don't let this man know the effect he's having on me.*

She duly blew out the candle and watched as the orange flame puffed out and a wisp of black smoke rose into the air.

Costa wondered what she had wished for. Not a new job, it would seem.

'Enjoy…' Costa said, and although he was irked that she had refused his offer, he was not enough of a bastard to leave her sitting alone with her single slice of birthday cake and two forks.

He picked up one of the forks. 'You go first.'

'Me?'

'It's *your* cake.'

Mary forgot for a moment how to do something as simple as pick up a fork and eat cake.

'Thank you,' she said finally, her breath returning. 'You're the first person to acknowledge my birthday…' Mary felt her blush fading as somewhat more normal service started to be resumed. 'I mean, in the scheme of things it's unimportant, but I've had not even a card or a single balloon…'

'I don't do cards.' He shrugged.

'What about balloons?'

He screwed up his nose.

'Well,' Mary said, more to herself than to him, 'it's not as if twenty-firsts are big birthdays any more...'

'I wish!' He rolled his eyes.

Now that he knew they would see each other no more, because she had not accepted his offer of the traineeship, it was as if he was letting her in just a touch.

'For mine there was a big party.'

She smiled.

'Not the sort of party you're imagining,' Costa told her. 'There was cake, which I don't like, photos, which I loathe, and I was reminded to appear grateful when my *yaya* presented me with my dead *papou*'s watch.'

'That's nice, isn't it?'

'My grandparents were not nice people.'

'You shouldn't speak ill of the dead.'

'You learn nothing from people's lives if you turn them into saints.' Costa shrugged. 'I still have to wear that damned watch whenever I'm home.'

'Lose it.' Mary leant forward and whispered the words. 'Perhaps wear it in the sea.'

And, unbeknownst even to her, Mary put on something she hadn't worn in the longest while—something forgotten, something long unseen. For Costa, she smiled her mettlesome smile.

'I like your line of thinking, Mary Jones,' he said. 'Here...'

He dived into the cake and offered her his loaded

fork. For a second it wobbled between them, as if for a sliver of time he'd been about to feed her.

It was enough to have her snapping back to attention, and she took the proffered fork from him and somehow guided it to her mouth.

'Mmm…' The sponge was so light, the cream like silk, and there was a burst of fresh strawberry on her tongue, both sweet and sharp. She was probably biased, but when her mouth was clear she said, 'This is the nicest cake I've ever tasted.'

'Really?'

He said it in that dubious tone Mary was coming to recognise, and she watched as he picked up the other fork and swooped in for a taste.

She couldn't help but stare.

Goodness, he was beyond handsome.

Those eyes were stunning, with thick, dark brows that framed them perfectly. She scanned his features, both in an attempt to find fault and, more honestly, to preserve this image of perfection, from the sculpted cheekbones to the strong unshaven jaw. And as for that mouth…

Mary was suddenly grateful that there was room in her stilettos for her toes to curl!

It was plump and open, and she watched that perfect cake disappear behind those perfect lips, leaving a slight smear of cream on the top one.

Oh, help.

She was beyond turned on, and it was such an unfamiliar feeling that she didn't know how to sit with it and just let it be. So distracted was she by the thrum of her veins beneath the grey tweed dress that she found herself mirroring him—licking her own top lip as he did the same.

Costa seemed a touch confounded as he went back for another taste. 'It is actually *very* nice.'

'You sound surprised?'

'I am,' he agreed. 'I really don't have a sweet tooth.'

'I'll have to remember that for future ref—' Her voice, which had gone all husky, stopped short.

Costa glanced up sharply. Yes, sharply. Because *sweet* Mary had just delivered a stunning and rather unexpected flirtation.

Rarely did flirting sideswipe Costa—he was an expert in it, after all. But he found that his guard was suddenly up.

The flush that had returned to her cheeks was now spreading down her neck, and it was not born of embarrassment or awkwardness. And her pupils were as big as the plate of cake they shared.

Well, not quite… But Costa recognised naked lust when he saw it.

Just who *was* this woman? In the space of an hour he had blown up long-held business plans, offered her a job, shared a birthday cake, and almost convinced himself that she was an innocent in this game called life.

It would seem he had been duped, for her eyes

told him there was something going on beneath her wide-eyed façade. He rarely felt rarely played when it came to seduction, but she might just be a master at it.

'There's no need for you to keep a record, Mary,' Costa said in rebuttal, 'given that we won't be seeing each other again.'

'Of course.'

All the cake was gone now, and this time when she reached for her purse he didn't stop her, though he did make himself stand.

'I'll walk you out.'

'Thank you.'

He knew she must have felt his sudden pulling back and, despite her inexperience, had understood why. The confusing part was that her flirtation had been unintentional and it seemed to have unsettled them both.

Yes, both.

Costa had been born flirting, and was rather certain he would take that skill to the grave. But tonight he really had been trying to do the right thing.

'Goodnight, Mary.'

'Goodnight.'

He knew he should turn to go, but instead he stood there, trying not to notice her shabby coat and the broken umbrella being handed to her as the doorman asked if he could summon her car or, when she declined, call a taxi.

'No, thank you...'

Mary had told him she had arrived by bus, and he guessed her mode of departure would be the same. He tried to remain unmoved. He had done his best, Costa told himself, and she had made it clear that she did not want his help.

But then, on some sort of reluctant autopilot—for he would by far prefer to walk away—he heard himself address the doorman. 'Could you arrange a car for Miss Jones, please?'

'Of course, sir.'

'It's fine,' Mary said. 'There really is no need.'

'I invited you for a drink,' Costa said as the car was swiftly arranged. 'I practically interviewed you. It is right that I ensure you get safely home.'

'I didn't accept the job,' Mary pointed out.

'As is your right. But that doesn't mean I leave you to take the bus.'

'Well, thank you.'

They stepped out into the cool evening to find that the rain had stopped but all was shiny and wet. For Mary, London had never looked so beautiful as it did this night.

It was as if everything had been swept clean. The terrible error of judgement she had made in accepting tonight's dinner date had been rectified and her birthday had been acknowledged.

It was almost like waking up to find the fairies had been while she slept.

She used to dream of that.

She used to fall asleep dreaming that she would wake up and her world would have changed. That her mother would be downstairs and her dad would be putting on a tie and heading to work. That the nightmare her childhood had become was just a dream from which she had finally awakened.

'Goodnight, Mary,' Costa said again. 'It was a pleasure to meet you.'

He said it so politely that for a moment she thought he might shake her hand, but he didn't, and when he spoke next there was a slight edge to his tone.

'I wish you well in whatever path you choose…'

His tone might be a little bit sarcastic, but she got why—given she had told him a little of her plight and then turned down such a stunning opportunity.

'Costa, I'm flattered by your offer. It really is the nicest proposal I've ever had. It's just that I have other commitments…'

'It was just a suggestion.'

'A very nice one,' Mary said. 'Thank you for thinking of me.' She swallowed. 'And for earlier…'

'No problem,' he lied.

She melted him.

Costa didn't quite know why.

There was a lot going on behind those china-blue eyes and thick honey lashes, and before he could think twice he cupped her cheeks with his hands in the gentlest of farewells as he offered his final warning.

'These other commitments…'

He still thought her an escort.

But even if it only served to compound his theory of her, she did not want to bring up her father.

'I don't want to discuss it.'

'Very well, but please be more careful in the future.'

'I am careful,' she countered.

Since her mother had died, she had been dreadfully so. She wanted to explain the aberration that tonight had been, but with her face in his hands there was no room for words, so she just carried on staring into those beautiful, inscrutable eyes.

'I mean it,' Costa said. 'There are a lot of snakes out there—believe me, I know…'

'How?' she asked.

'Because I've had to work with them. For a while I was one of them.'

She wanted to know more.

Mary wanted more.

It was as though he was a magnet and her skin was embedded with shards of iron. She was drawn to him. So much so that she had to press her soles into the floor to ground herself and tell her lips not to move towards his.

Costa could feel the shiver of anticipation beneath his fingers and he looked at the perfect lips he had watched blow out a candle. He wanted them on his, yet he reminded himself of the circumstances of their meeting.

No, to kiss her now would not be fair.

He removed his hands from her burning cheeks.

'I am going back in.'

Yet still he could not leave things there.

'If I wanted to call you…?' Costa checked, and saw her eyes widen. 'I think it would be poor form to ask Ridgemont for your details.'

'Indeed.'

'So,' he said, 'what is your number?'

He took out his phone and, oh, so confidently went to type it in.

'I don't have one,' Mary said.

She gave him a brittle smile as it dawned on her that he might be considering booking her 'services', before remembering that he'd said he didn't pay for company.

'I think it best we leave it there.'

'Certainly,' Costa said, pocketing his phone.

'You have your party to get to.'

'No,' Costa corrected as he saw her into his car. 'That was just to get rid of Ridgemont. I'm going back in now…' He gestured with his head to the hotel. 'Happy birthday, Mary.'

He closed the car door and watched as it glided out into the dark night.

'Is everything all right, sir?' the doorman asked.

'Of course.' Costa nodded, for now she was gone he could finally think straight.

As he went back inside Costa mentally amended his response.

In fact, things were far from okay.

In fact, the night had not gone well at all.

Somehow Mary Jones had not just blown up his carefully laid plans, she had completely upended him.

CHAPTER FOUR

MARY JONES HAD upended more than Costa's evening. She had disrupted his sleep. For, despite having his preferred suite in his preferred hotel, rest had not come easily.

Costa opened the drapes long before dawn and lay in bed, watching the steady beat of rain on the windows. He thought of her out there...

Adrift.

The word had unsettled him—for, no, he did not know that feeling.

Be it on a fishing boat in the centre of the heaviest storm, or sleeping on a Santorini beach having missed the last ferry home, he had always felt anchored. Weighted down by responsibility, perhaps, but he had never felt alone.

Chance would be a fine thing, Costa thought wryly, as at that very second the 'do not disturb' function on his phone automatically turned itself off, and the phone buzzed with a ringtone that denoted it was his mother.

Now what? It was earlier here in London, but

even in Anapliró it was still an ungodly hour for a Sunday. Or rather a Godly hour, because most of the locals would be making their way to church.

'Who is she?' his mother demanded.

'What are you going on about?' Costa groaned.

'Angela asked when she brought me my breakfast... You'll be the talk of the village today. Poor Roula...'

'Roula?' Costa needed half a litre of coffee before he dealt with the rapid fire of his mother's questions. 'What the hell does Roula have to do with this?'

'Oh, come off it, Costa. You are looking at this woman with such affection... It's all over the internet...'

She fired him a link and he fought not to groan, for he and Mary had been photographed outside the hotel, her face cupped in his hands, seemingly a second away from a kiss that had not actually happened.

'So?' his mother demanded.

'Leave it, Yolanda,' Costa said, for he had long since called his mother by her first name.

'No. I can just picture Nemo sulking if he finds out that you are serious about someone...' Nemo was Roula's brother and Costa's head of security at the retreat. 'You two are promised to each other—'

'I'm not discussing this,' Costa cut in. 'We'll speak later.'

'Surely you can give me her name? Everyone will be asking. Of course, if it's no one serious…'

'Enjoy church,' Costa said, for he could hear the bells in the background. 'I'll see you in Athens for your birthday.'

'But that is what I'm calling about! There has been a cancellation next weekend at the retreat—that big corporate booking…'

'I don't need to know…' He closed his eyes in frustration; his mother still didn't get that he didn't need to know such details. 'You don't need to call me about every booking or cancellation. I own it—I don't run it…'

'No, Costa, listen. I have decided to have my fiftieth in Anapliró.'

Costa sat up in bed abruptly, not liking what he was hearing but keeping his voice even. 'We're having dinner in Athens,' Costa reminded her.

In fact, it was far more than dinner. Costa had taken more than a year to plan and execute her gift—not that his mother knew.

'Anyway, you can't organise a party in a week.'

'It wouldn't be any trouble for a paying guest.'

Of course it wouldn't be—and in truth, the gift he had planned for his mother would be far better delivered on the island. Except he had been avoiding going there for so long…

'I want this, Costa,' his mother said.

Costa knew exactly what his mother wanted—and so many others on the island too—for the prodigal son to return and for past decisions to be erased. It was about more than Costa. It was about traditions and family honour and all he sought to escape.

He knew the pressure his mother was under, for he had felt the claws of it himself during occasional brief visits.

'I want to celebrate how far we have come,' Yolanda continued. 'I want to be surrounded by friends and to stand with my son. I want my birthday here...'

Anapliró.

Costa was being summoned home.

CHAPTER FIVE

'HOW WAS YOUR BIRTHDAY, Mary?'

Sitting opposite her father on her regular Monday afternoon visit, she thought that precious time with Costa seemed light years away.

'It was fine.' Mary pushed out a smile.

'What did you get up to?'

She tried to come up with something, but no words were forthcoming. 'Just...'

Mary couldn't explain to her father, let alone herself, what had transpired. Not the awful part, nor the job offer, not even the cake...

'How's work?' Her father broke into her thoughts and perhaps read them a little. 'No luck with the apprenticeship?'

'No.' She told him a little of what was going on in her world. 'Coral gave it to the daughter of a friend.'

'You've still got a job, though?' he checked.

'Yes...' Mary took a breath. The glimmer of confidence she had found in speaking with Costa felt almost snuffed out now, but she was fighting to reignite it. 'I'm applying elsewhere, though. I went to the library this morning and found a book on writing a CV.'

'That's good.' Her father looked at her. 'Mary, you know I love seeing you, but I don't want to hold you back…'

'Dad, please don't.'

She did not want to hear again how he'd prefer it if she didn't come and how he loathed her seeing him here.

There was a dreadful stretch of silence then, and still a full fifty minutes to go. Both knew what the other was thinking.

About that fateful night.

'I'm so sorry, Mary…'

'Dad, please…' Mary shrivelled into herself, for it was something she simply could not think about, let alone sit and discuss.

And so they sat in silence.

Yet as she looked at her frail father, once so dependable and strong, every moment of that night played like a magic lantern on the walls of her mind.

Her grandmother had come over to babysit while her parents attended a function. Mary had been in trouble again, and was to have been sent to bed early with no treats.

'No treats!' Granny Farrell had exclaimed. *'Why not?'*

'Because Mary has to learn,' her dad had said.

He'd come over and knelt down beside her and taken her clenched hands in his. *'You can't just go running off like you did.'*

'I know.'

'Mary, what you did was extremely dangerous...' He'd looked over to her mum. *'Perhaps we should give tonight a miss.'*

'She'll be fine,' her mum had said as she'd picked up the car keys. *'Anyway, we won't be long. We'll just put in an appearance.'*

'But Mary's upset.'

'Then she needs a night with Granny. Come on, darling, or we'll be late.'

There had been the swirl of her mum's dress as she'd crossed the room, the familiar floral scent as she'd bent over and kissed her pinched face, which had been blotchy from crying.

'There are some treats,' her mum had whispered as she'd wrapped Mary in her arms. *'Let Granny think she found them. I love you, darling.'*

Fourteen years on, Mary could still feel the tender, fragrant shelter of her mother's embrace, which was denied to her for ever now.

It was a relief when visiting time ended.

There was no sign of spring as she stepped out into the rain, just grey upon grey. Even the red bus looked grimy as it approached, and Mary was jostled as she stepped on. There were no seats, so she stood holding on to the back of one, jolting with each stop-start lurch. As they turned into the high street and neared her stop, all Mary wanted to do was get in the shower and... Not just wash away the prison smell, but to cry in a way that she hadn't since her mother's funeral.

But Mary was scared that if she started she might never stop.

She was still so very hurt by and cross with her father, but there could be nothing gained by revealing that to him. Mary knew he was depressed, and blamed himself for the accident, and knew of the downward spiral he had fallen into afterwards.

The worst part—the unsaid part—was that she also blamed him.

How she wanted to be back there in the lounge of that hotel now, sipping hot chocolate and talking... Being listened to.

Costa had actually sat down with her and taken the time to consider her options—had offered her work.

In that slice of time she had felt *seen*.

But even before that thought had been properly processed Mary amended it, for suddenly all she wanted to do was remain unseen. She wanted nothing more than to hide.

For Costa Leventis was stepping out of a luxury car similar to the one that had taken her home the other night.

Mary didn't exactly dress up when she visited her father in prison, and she was horribly aware of her thick black tights and the even thicker jumper over a denim skirt—all drenched, of course.

Naturally he looked stunning, in a long, dark coat and shoes that made her think of Sir Walter Raleigh putting down his cloak for the Queen. He was rakishly unshaven, Mary noted uncomfortably. It was as though the devil himself had come to her door—except it wasn't terror that had her stomach tightening as he approached.

'What are you doing here?'

'I booked in for a trim.'

'We're closed on Mondays,' Mary said, and took out her keys.

'So how come you're working?'

'Just catching up while it's quiet,' she responded, too embarrassed to admit she lived there. 'Now, if you'll excuse me, I need to get on.'

'I have a proposal to put to you.'

'I said no.'

'A different one.'

'No, thank you!' Mary answered tartly.

She couldn't bear it that he thought she charged by the hour. Except she didn't unlock the door and go inside. Costa challenged her at every level. He was the most perfect sight for sore eyes, and the most exciting, unexpected moment of her dreary day.

'It's a serious proposal. If you would rather I don't come in, of course that's fine, but can we at least go somewhere more conducive to conversation? I don't have much time...'

She knew she should just end this now—except it was as if her heart had been waiting to see him again, and she was curious as to what he had to say.

'Very well.' Mary nodded and unlocked the salon door. 'But just for a moment…'

She felt as if she should apologise in advance for her rather tawdry living conditions, but then she remembered he didn't know that she lived there.

Eftelis.

That was Costa's first thought as he entered the salon to the jangle of a bell and looked around. It was tacky, garish, and everything Mary was not.

She does not belong here, was his second.

'May I sit?' he asked politely.

'Please do.'

And although he sat in a chair in which perhaps a thousand others had also sat, Costa did not blend in. He was just too much man for the salon. She imagined the flurry if he were to walk in from the street on a work day…

'Please don't make this a habit,' Mary told him. 'I doubt my boss will be pleased if I have friends dropping by.'

'I am glad you consider me a friend,' Costa answered smoothly.

'I meant—'

'I know what you meant. Don't worry—I have no intention of ever coming here again.'

Mary felt her nostrils pinch, for there was a slight

warning behind his words that told her this man would never make a pest of himself.

It told her, too, that she had better listen—that this opportunity, this 'proposal' would not be made more than once. Costa Leventis was not a man who repeated himself.

She chose to stand as he angled the faux leather chair to face her. His coat fell open and beneath it she saw he was wearing a dark suit and crisp white shirt with a gunmetal-grey tie...

Quite simply, he thrilled her.

'You have created quite a stir online,' Costa told her. 'I assume you've seen the gossip?'

'What gossip?'

'People are asking "Who is she?" because there is a photo circulating online of us outside the hotel. You really haven't seen it?'

Mary gave a slight shake of her head. 'I don't have a mobile phone. I told you.'

To Costa it was as if she were in some kind of time warp, separate from the world around her...

Her arms were folded and at any moment, Costa knew, she would be ready to tell him to get the hell out.

Mary confused him: she was well-spoken and evidently clever, and yet she could not secure an apprenticeship. And she was so wary... Yet given the nature of her second job she was clearly adventurous too.

Her blonde hair was dark from the rain and un-brushed today, but her blue eyes were so vivid that each time they met his there was an element of surprise. For they were the colour of the Aegean Sea. Not the Aegean he could see from his Athens high-rise—her eyes were the colour of the Aegean on a summer's day in Anapliró.

'Your name is apt,' he said now.

'Is it?'

'I remember when I learnt English at school there was a rhyme—"Mary, Mary, Quite Contrary". I was eight or so, and had no idea what *contrary* meant.'

He looked at her innocent and yet not so innocent eyes, her full lips and her absolutely unspoiled beauty, and he knew that she kept secrets.

'I am starting to understand the meaning a little better now…'

'I don't think you came here to discuss nursery rhymes.'

'Of course not. I am here because I have just found out that I am to return to Anapliró at the weekend for my mother's fiftieth…'

'Fiftieth!' Mary said. 'Gosh, she must have had you—' Costa's deliberate eyebrow raise served to halt her. He did not need the all too familiar judgment as to how old his mother must have been when she'd had him.

'Yolanda has suddenly decided she wants a

party, and naturally wants me there.' He noticed her frown as he referred to his mother by her first name. 'I've been giving it some thought and I have decided it would be easier all round if I bring someone...'

Costa was being so direct that there was no room in Mary's mind for any flight of fantasy that he was asking her on a date.

'There is an ex of sorts,' Costa went on. 'And my return will raise expectations—not just from my mother, but from the islanders too. They all want to get involved in my life and I just want them off my back. My bringing you to the party would achieve that. At the very least it would shut them down for a while.'

'Don't you have a lover you could take?'

'Not one who wouldn't read too much into it— whereas you and I have no romantic history, so there are no illusions to shatter.'

Mary chose not to correct him, or to reveal that she'd actually been spinning romantic illusions about him since they'd parted on Saturday night.

Not now.

For there was nothing romantic about what he proposed.

He hadn't even prettied things up by arriving with flowers. Instead, he had no issue in getting straight to the unsavoury point.

'You would be well compensated.'

'I thought you never paid for company?'

'I don't,' he agreed. 'But on this occasion there is definite appeal. Yolanda is a white witch—she would spot a fake date a mile off.'

'I *would* be a fake date, though.'

'Of course, but you are...different,' he said.

It was exactly what people tended to whisper behind her back—or at times said outright to her face. Except he did not say it unkindly...so much so that she wondered if it was the smooth silk of his voice that made it sound almost like a compliment.

'Different?' She checked the word again, just in case he might want to amend it.

'Refreshingly so,' he admitted, and swung a little in the chair.

Costa was trying to fathom what it was about Mary that muddled his brain. Her beauty was a given, but if that were the sole criteria there were many beautiful women he could take.

There was something about her that intrigued him. Like a magazine quiz he might take in an idle moment, only to find the answers torn out when he turned to find them at the back.

'Okay, I need to bring more than a date,' Costa said. 'It needs to look as if we're serious—and, thanks to the photo now circulating in the media, you're already the talk of Anapliró.'

He held out his phone and she took it and stared silently at the image of them on the screen.

'Your face is obscured, so don't worry.'

Right now, Mary wasn't worried about being recognised. She was entirely consumed by how the image had captured the moment, and the look in Costa's eyes as he stared down at her.

It must be a trick of the light, she told herself, or the angle of the camera, but they looked so intimate…as if they were lovers indeed.

'It's not possible.' Her voice was a little croaky as she handed him back his phone. 'I'd be fired if I took time off at short notice. We can't all drop everything in our lives to hop onto a private jet.'

'Sorry to disappoint,' Costa said, 'but I don't believe in private jets. You'd be flying commercial.' His voice softened. 'If your boss would fire you merely for having a life, might I suggest that you need this more than ever.'

His words gave her pause.

'I have thought about what you said about feeling adrift,' he continued, 'and I understand that you might not want to move to Greece to work, but a long weekend in Anapliró could mean a whole new start.'

He told her the whole deal then. How her wardrobe, travel and accessories would 'naturally' be accounted for. But it was the cash figure he offered that had her frowning.

'Not enough?' Costa checked, as if this was a negotiating tactic.

But she watched his cynicism dim with her next words.

'Costa, it would change my life.'

It truly would. For it was enough to pay for accommodation while she looked for other work. Enough to get the hell out of this place and for the first time in her adult life to breathe without fear. But…

'You yourself warned me to be more careful,' she told him. 'How do I know that I'm not just walking straight back into trouble?'

'I can have it all put in writing if you so choose.'

'As if that would help me!' Mary gave a hollow laugh. 'I'm sure you have a team of lawyers at your disposal.'

'Perhaps, but although this is strictly a business deal, I have ensured that it benefits us both.'

For so many years Mary had chosen to stay quiet, but with him she more easily found her voice, and now she said what she guessed few would ever dare. 'I imagine you once said the same to Eric Ridgemont. Have you told him yet that you're pulling out of whatever deal it is you agreed with him?'

'That's none of your business.'

'Actually, it is.' Mary watched a muscle leap in his cheek, but he didn't scare her the way Eric had, or Coral did, or the way life tended to at times. 'Isn't a gentleman's word supposed to be his bond?'

He nodded curtly.

'From where I was sitting the other night, it looked as if Eric was about to get badly burnt.'

'Forget it,' Costa said, and abruptly stood up. He felt as though she had her teeth lodged in his Achilles' heel. 'It was just a suggestion. Thank you for your time.'

But Mary was a brand of trouble he had never before encountered, for instead of stalking out he found himself pausing. Then he turned around.

'I have just come from meeting Ridgemont and, yes, I have told him. I don't generally go back on my word.'

'I can only go on what I've seen.'

'I have my reasons.'

He was aware that she had seen him poised with a wrecking ball on Saturday night. The same wrecking ball he had delivered this very afternoon. But while she was right to question him—and he admired her for it—Costa was hesitant to answer her.

'I have never discussed this with another living soul,' he said at last.

Mary knew that feeling only too well. 'We all have our secrets.'

He looked at those stunning blue eyes and knew

she was asking him to trust her. He felt compelled to find it within himself to do it.

'You were right about us going back further than fifteen years.' He paused, still so loath to share his sordid past. 'What you don't know, and neither does he, is that he walked over my mother.'

'Meaning?'

'Exactly that. I was working at a marina. My mother worked there too, and she had an attack.' He saw Mary frown and explained. 'She has MS, and for the first time she had lost her vision. It was temporary—not that she knew that at the time. She collapsed. Your boyfriend just stepped over her body on the ground.'

'Please don't call him that.'

'Your *client*, then.'

And now her eyes were as blue as the midday sky of home, and he was right back there, reliving that day.

'He just stepped right over her,' Costa repeated. 'I called for water and he didn't even turn. In fact, he and his friends laughed. Their yacht had a doctor, its own helicopter, and yet they just let her lie there. And then, when no help arrived, they had Security move her because their guests were arriving. She messed with the aesthetics, I suppose. I have hated him for a very long time.'

'Yet you do business with him?'

'I do,' Costa agreed. 'Or rather, until this afternoon I *did*. There are a lot of deals made on those yachts, and I taught myself to play his filthy game in order to beat him at it.'

So far this experience was proving less cathartic than he had hoped. Instead it was making his guts burn.

'I was always going to cut loose, though, and I was very much looking forward to severing all contact the other night. But then, dear Mary, I'd have left him all to *you*.'

Mary blinked, taking it all in, yet still wanting to know much more, but clearly Costa had already said way more than he'd intended to.

'It's one long weekend,' he told her. 'And you'd have most of it to yourself.'

'To myself?'

'Friday we'll be on Thira, sorting out your wardrobe and getting our stories straight…'

'Thira?'

'Santorini.'

'But I thought you lived in Athens?'

'Santorini is where we will sort out the things a serious partner would know—for, believe me, the whole island will be watching me with my outsider…'

'Outsider?'

'You.'

Mary shrugged, despite how much it hurt to be described this way. 'I am always an outsider.'

'Not to me. And I'll be with you.'

'How would we say we met?'

'We'll deal with that later…' Costa said dismissively, but then appeared to give it some thought. 'Best we stick close to the truth and say you were dating a mutual acquaintance…'

He shrugged.

'Friday evening we would fly to Anapliró, to say a quick hello to my mother.' He held up one finger. 'You can spend the day as you like until the party on Saturday night.' He held up another. 'I am spending the day with her on Sunday.' He did not raise a third finger. 'There's no need to for you to come along.'

'I might want to come along.'

Costa actually gave a half-laugh. He obviously thought she was joking.

'You would have the entire day to yourself.' He raised a third finger. 'We'd fly back to Athens on Sunday night, and from there you would return to London.'

While he made it sound so straightforward, clean and above board, Mary hated how much it made her sound like a paid escort. Inwardly she laughed wryly at the fact that she'd never so much as been kissed by a man, save for that wretched slobber from Eric the other night…

'Look, I know you must think…' She didn't know how best to put it. Her cheeks were scalding. 'I mean, when we met—'

'I understand that you are trying to change your

life,' Costa cut in. 'I really mean it when I say that I am only paying for your acting skills. I need a devoted girlfriend in public. The fact we have chemistry only serves to make it more believable...'

'Chemistry?' Mary checked, because that was the very thing she had been attempting to hide, yet he simply stated it upfront.

'*élxi,*' Costa stated it in Greek, for her bewilderment had him momentarily wondering about his choice of word in English. Certainly he did not doubt for a second the energy that thrummed between them. 'Lure' was what he settled for. 'I find you beautiful, and there is no denying that we are attracted to each other. I mean, look at the photo!'

Though Mary stood stock-still, there was no denying it. And she didn't need to see the photo again to confirm the *something* that had nearly occurred the other night.

Was still occurring.

His scent was subtle, yet its notes were already familiar, and she felt an odd craving to move closer to him. And although his eyes never left her face, the effect of his silvery gaze set off an internal cascade, as if plump velvet dominos were quietly falling. She felt each pump of blood in her veins and the spread of warmth beneath her damp clothing, as well as a choking awareness that she had never encountered before.

Until him.

'However...' Costa broke into her dangerous thoughts '... I am certainly not paying for sex.'

'Oh.'

She felt suddenly and most curiously deflated. As if every fizzing cell that had been happily bounding towards unknown and uncharted territories had suddenly ground to an abrupt halt.

'And you don't have to worry,' he continued blithely. 'I loathe PDAs, so I won't be all over you. We would have to dance, of course, and they would expect that we'd kiss now and then, but that would be all.'

'And no sex?'

'I didn't say that.'

He looked right at her then, and the look was so potent that it stripped her. Not just of her clothes; she felt suddenly translucent—as though he could see right inside her and witness her tightening desire.

'I'm not sure I know what you mean...' Mary croaked.

'Then I'll make it very clear: apart from when we have an audience present, I won't lay a finger on you.'

'And when the audience is not present?'

'The same,' Costa said. 'You either want me or you don't.'

'And if I don't?'

'I have a guest suite in my villa.'

'Wouldn't the maids think it odd...?'

'I don't give a damn what they think. Maybe that I snore?'

'And if…?' She felt a little giddy, baffled that she was even attempting to say what she was about to. 'And if I do…?'

'Then you come to me.'

Her throat squeezed tight on the breath she tried to drag in, for Mary could not fathom ever being so bold.

And yet…and yet…

'Any other questions?' he demanded, perhaps a little sarcastically.

Hiring an escort should surely not be so complicated, he thought. Still, he had done his best to put her at ease, but now he really did need to get on.

'I can arrange an airport hotel for Thursday, and you'd depart early Friday morning.'

'We wouldn't fly together?'

'Fly together?' He gave a bemused frown. 'No. I'm heading to the airport now.'

'But you said you were here all week.'

'Mary, if we do meet to get our stories straight, there is one thing you should know about me: I don't run my plans, nor any changes I make to them, by anyone.'

'Poor her, then,' Mary said to his departing back as that awful bell jangled when he opened the door.

'Poor who?'

'Your real partner,' Mary said, and he turned

around. 'The one who has to keep the "for future reference" book on you.'

'There will never be one.'

'Never?' Mary asked.

'Never, ever,' Costa said and, eternally wary, decided to make very sure. He closed the door. 'You *are* clear that there is nothing more to this than a temporary arrangement, aren't you?'

'I'm just…' She looked up at him. 'I'm just interested, that's all. You really don't want someone in your life?'

'I don't,' Costa agreed. 'Being beholden to no one is my sole aim.'

'Wow!' Mary blinked. 'That sounds a whole lot better than being adrift. I might have to try it.'

'Do,' Costa said and, although he really should have been long since gone, there was a certain pleasure in her company that made him linger just a little while more. 'There is a saying in Greece—*gia parti mou*. It's my party. It means doing something for yourself, taking care of yourself, putting yourself first. I highly recommend it.'

'I shall take it on board,' Mary said, and this time it was she who opened the door for him.

'Try it!' Costa said as his driver jumped out of the car and walked at pace to open the door and then hopefully get Costa to the airport in the nick of time.

He lingered for a fraction of a second too long,

and then gave in to the thought that had been ruling his head since Saturday night.

Her hair was almost dry now, and bunched in unruly waves—just the way it might look on his pillow.

If she ever came to him.

He still could not read Mary. He had seen her gorgeous eyes light up with desire, and he had seen her turn, ready to run, that first night when she had thought he offered sex.

There was so much going on beneath the surface, Costa knew. But there was a lot at stake for him this weekend, and he needed to be sure that their arrangement would work.

'Perhaps we should try a couple of practice kisses,' Costa said now. 'Just so we know that you won't do a Ridgemont on me…'

'A Ridgemont?'

'You flinched when he touched you. We can't risk that happening…'

'When he kissed me at the table, you mean?'

'That wasn't a kiss,' Costa corrected. 'That was gross.'

Mary swallowed. She had no point of reference, but she was glad to have confirmation that her instinctive reaction had been appropriate.

'What are you doing?' she asked as he tugged down the bell on the door and it clattered to the floor.

'It fell,' he told her. 'Perhaps tell your boss

she's incredibly lucky that a customer wasn't hurt when it did.'

Now there was the bliss of silence when he closed the door.

'My jumper's wet…and your shirt…'

Why she was worried for his shirt, Mary wasn't sure.

'It's a kiss,' he said, and for the second time in their short history he took her face in his hands.

She stared up at him and watched that gorgeous mouth.

'I don't detect any flinching.'

Mary was trembling on the inside, though. His palms were at the edge of her jaw, his gorgeous fingers lightly over her ears, and then his mouth found the spot, the *exact* spot, where the awful Eric had kissed her.

She closed her eyes at the softness of his mouth and it was as if the fairies had been again, wiping the spot clean, annulling that kiss from history. Because, with the lightest of touches from his velvet lips, Costa Leventis kissed her first.

'Would you like me to fetch a towel so you can wipe your cheek?' Costa asked, and she smiled, for he had clearly noticed what she'd done at the table.

'No need.'

And then the world went silver as his mouth moved to hers, and with the weight of his lips Mary amended everything.

This was her first kiss.

It was like being stroked with a feather, soothing and tautening her simultaneously. The brush of his lips made her ache for more, and as she opened her mouth to gasp there came the shock of his cool tongue and the slow slide of it in her mouth. It made her want to lean deeper into him, to brush the wedge of muscle with her own. Yet all she was capable of doing was standing there, as she was very slowly, very delectably, very deeply kissed.

And then it ended.

From his expression she thought she was the only one affected.

'I think we're good to go,' Costa said.

'I haven't said yes yet.'

'But you are thinking about it.'

Oh, she was. Her mind was darting, exhilaration returning as he held her.

'I really do have to go,' he told her and let her go.

Good, because Mary needed to think.

'I shall see you on Thira,' Costa said.

And as she opened her mouth to remind him that she hadn't yet made up her mind, he spoke over her.

'Or not. It is entirely up to you.'

CHAPTER SIX

MARY HADN'T EXACTLY been expecting Costa to stand holding flowers and balloons as she stepped into Arrivals in Santorini. But then, given the enormity of her decision and its ramifications, neither had she expected a gorgeous, rather bored, rather pregnant woman in a tight blue dress, holding a sign with her name on, to be there to greet her.

'I'm Mary…' She made herself known while biting back foolish disappointment.

'I thought so.' The woman didn't even bother to smile, just looked at her trolley, with her old rucksack and the bag from Mary's first ever splurge in Duty Free. 'I'm Kristina—Galen's PA.'

'Galen?'

'Don't worry about it…' She waved her question away. 'There's been a change of plan. It slipped Costa's mind that you were coming and he only told me a short while ago.'

If her rather harsh upbringing and many late-night arrivals in new foster homes had taught Mary anything it was not to expect a warm welcome, but even with a generous allowance for the words being 'lost in translation', this hurt.

Not that Mary would ever let it show.

Still, the fact that one of the biggest, most difficult decisions of her life—one that had cost her her job and her home—had been but an afterthought to Costa was sobering indeed.

'Take it up with Costa.' Kristina shrugged. She muttered something in Greek, and then needlessly translated. 'Arrogant bastard.'

So Mary had been told.

'Oh, and you're to give me your bank details,' Kristina added. 'I'll sort out a transfer this morning.'

At that moment Mary could happily have killed Costa, but she stammered out something about not being comfortable giving out such personal information.

'We've never met,' Mary pointed out to Kristina. 'How do I know it's not a scam?'

'You think Costa Leventis wants to scam *your* bank account!' Kristina laughed to herself, only not in a very nice way. 'Is there anything you need from your bag before we put it in the car?'

Retrieving her shiny new contraceptive pills and her fridge magnet—as the immaculate but very bored Kristina looked on—was an exercise in humiliation.

The whole morning was.

With each passing moment Mary methodically retrieved and discarded all the little arrows Costa had lodged in her heart and mentally grounded all flights of fancy. She was so disappointed by Costa's no-show that even the bright sun left her disenchanted.

It was time for some more dreaded small talk. 'Gosh, it's warmer than I expected...'

'False summer,' Kristina said.

Mary attempted no more.

Santorini's marina was brimming with gorgeousness when they arrived there, but Mary felt numb as Kristina told her the plans for the day.

'Leo will sort out your wardrobe.'

Mary frowned. 'Leo?'

'Leo Arati.'

Even Mary had heard of him. He dressed the rich and the beautiful who featured in the salon's magazines, which she pored over at night, but she felt no real joy at the thought of being dressed by such an icon.

'First, though,' Kristina said, 'let's get you to the salon.'

'I thought there was one on Anapliró.'

'You need a complete makeover prior to your arrival there.'

Kristina's brusque manner offended Mary too easily. And so did the salon girls as they discussed with Kristina all that needed to be done. Mary was taken off to be pummelled and waxed—though certainly not *there*, she told them. And even before she got to her first ever scalp massage with a deep conditioning treatment she no longer craved it.

Frankly, even Coral was kinder.

Only it wasn't really Kristina who upset her, nor the salon girls. There was just nothing fun or romantic about being groomed to meet 'the master'.

It was romance and fun that she craved, but she dislodged a few more arrows and just sat there, shrivelled into herself, as she always tended to, and watched silently as her hair was expertly cut and dried.

Mary thought she was over Costa before the weekend had started. But then came kindness from a most unexpected source in the tiny frame of Leo Arati. He was shorter even than Mary, and elegantly bald with huge silver earrings. As she entered the small studio he tried to embrace her rigid body in a hug, but when Mary resisted he let her go.

Kristina said something to him in Greek, but Leo wasn't listening.

'Adio.' He snapped, and then pulled a face as Kristina left. 'She kills me.' He rolled his eyes dramatically. 'She tries to tell Leo Arati how to dress you.'

'Yes,' Mary said. 'She tried to suggest I go copper.'

'No, no…' He pulled out a ream of fabric and held it next to her. 'Not your colour.'

Mary had been talking about Kristina's suggestion for her hair, but it really didn't matter.

'Costa is such a bastard,' said Leo.

'Yes.'

'But…' He shrugged. 'Then he smiles and all is forgiven.'

Not by Mary.

Still, at least Leo did his best to put her at ease with his constant chatter, even if neither understood much of what the other said.

'Sunny, sunny!' He smiled. 'All week!'

'Isn't it always?'

'Not usually now. Early summer, maybe. You swim?'

'No…' Mary shook her head.

'So this…?' He held up the tiniest bikini, which was really just ribbons.

'No, no!' Mary shook her head. 'I can't possibly wear that…'

'For sure!'

He insisted she try it on, but then he must have seen the defeat in her face as she stared at her pale reflection and tried to cover herself with her hands.

'This one,' Leo said, and held up something marginally safer; and when he showed her how to tie a flimsy little sarong over it she felt somewhat better.

As Mary tried things on, Leo pinned and his assistant took care of alterations as they moved on to the next item.

'Perfect,' Leo said as he checked the alterations on a party dress they had chosen in the palest gold. 'You will kill them.'

Given he'd said much the same about Kristina,

Mary wasn't sure if that was a compliment, though it was such a gorgeous dress she chose to take it as one.

And, even with their communication limited, she found out more about the weekend ahead than Costa had shared.

'Yolanda…' Leo said with a mouthful of pins. 'Busy, busy.'

'Okay.'

'And Roula…' He sighed. 'Poor Roula.'

Mary frowned at the familiar name, for she had heard Costa on his phone to her.

'Why "poor Roula"?' Mary asked casually.

But instead of elaborating Leo gave her exclusive access to his summer collection of the sheerest, most glorious underwear.

'These,' Leo urged, holding up a gorgeous, provocative violet set which even had a name. 'This year's Sófisma collection. Deception,' he translated.

And deceptive she would indeed be, wearing something so overtly sexy, and she settled for a few sets that were a little less…well, *daring*.

Flesh colour was surely safe, Mary thought as she alighted on another set.

'Love!' Leo said. 'It is the My Hope Dies Tonight collection.' Mary blinked at the appalling name and realised Leo must have seen her reaction when he added, 'It sounds better in Greek…'

This was the first studio he had owned, she gleaned, and…

'Costa was my model,' Leo told her as they waited for the dress chosen for her to wear today to be taken in. 'A long time ago.'

'I can't imagine Costa on a catwalk!'

'Catwalk? No.' Leo shook his head. 'I gave up design school. Costa has the Midas touch, so I paid his bar bill in return for him wearing my clothes out there...' He gestured to the fashionable world of Santorini outside, which she had only briefly glimpsed. 'Then on Mykonos, and then...'

He stopped his reminiscence, though she wished he'd continue, but her dress was finally ready so she put it on.

'Then?' Mary asked as he helped with the hidden zip. And even though there had been a gap in conversation, from his smile they both knew she referred to the 'then' after Mykonos.

He gave her no answer, though. 'Look at you!'

Mary stared at her reflection and barely recognised herself. She wore a pale mint shift dress, but it was not just a shift dress, for the hem and seams were visible and had been sewn in the palest gold thread, as had the butter-soft ballet pumps.

'I thought you were going to cut the gold thread off,' Mary admitted; she had assumed it was tacking.

'For sure!' Leo smiled. 'You'll kill them.'

'Indeed she shall...'

The deep voice aimed a fresh arrow to her heart, but she yanked it out before she looked up. The arrow that was lodged straight in her pelvis remained, however, for Costa looked both terrible and stunning all at the same time.

Bruised, sulking, rumpled…

Her imagination ran riot, for he looked as if he'd just come off worse in some crazy fight in a casino, or fallen off a horse, but if that was the case why would he be wearing black trousers and a white shirt?

'What happened?' Mary asked, even as her mind danced with a million possibilities.

That aquiline nose had not been broken, for she could see it was perfectly straight, but she guessed he hadn't shaved since their last meeting, for it was more than a couple of days' growth he wore; it was practically a beard.

He was here, and as utterly beautiful as she remembered, yet he was more unpredictable than she could allow.

'Much longer, Leo?' he asked, instead of enlightening Mary.

'All done.' Leo smiled.

Costa thanked him in Greek, and Leo, who had been so kind to her, snapped something back.

'Leo has a party to get to,' Costa said, and so it was he who wheeled her new luggage out.

They walked in silence. Mary was cross and he was clearly exhausted. So much so that he closed his eyes when they took a seat at a taverna, and didn't even open them to speak to an attentive waiter, just nodded to whatever he was offered.

A drink, it would seem, for two glasses were put down and liquor instantly poured.

When Mary declined, Costa snapped himself out of his reverie. 'What would you like?' he asked.

'Nothing,' Mary sulked.

He shook his head to the waiter, who drifted off.

She watched as he took up a carafe of water and added it to the liquor, which turned from clear to milky.

'Would you like to order a drink before I apologise? I'd like to do it without the waiter here.'

'Iced chocolate milk.'

'Good.' He called out her order and then took a drink.

'Is that Pernod?' Mary asked, because she'd heard of that and how it went cloudy.

'Ouzo.' He frowned at the irrelevance of her question, but glanced over at her. 'Do you want to try it?'

He pushed the glass towards her and she felt a shiver.

Because he had no problem with sharing his glass.

Such a tiny thing to him.

An absolute first for her.

'No, thank you.'

'Look… I am sorry I wasn't there to greet you. I was held up, so I called Kristina and asked her to meet you.'

'You also told her to take my bank details,' Mary sneered.

It was something she never usually did, but Costa

brought out something in her—something old, something new, something borrowed, maybe, but not something blue. Costa Leventis made her see red.

'How tacky!'

Mary stopped talking as the waiter approached with her drink. Costa waited until they were alone before responding. He rarely explained himself, but in this case he felt he owed her at least part of an explanation.

'I asked her to get your details in case I couldn't be here,' Costa said, meeting her gaze.

He'd wanted the money side of things sorted—wanted one less thing to worry about. Because where Mary was concerned he felt suddenly cheap, like some sleazy old man. 'I didn't want you to feel stranded or trapped.'

'I have an emergency fund,' Mary told him, '*and* an open return ticket,' she added with a thinly veiled warning as to where this was leading. 'But after insulting me, Kristina took me to a beauty salon, and then on to Leo.'

'So I see.'

He still hadn't commented on her clothes and hair; he knew he ought to because she looked stunning. But then he'd thought she was stunning on Saturday night too.

'You look beautiful, by the way.'

'By the way?' Mary let out a half-laugh at this rather underwhelming response to her head-to-toe make-

over; the events of this morning still stung. 'So I'm Costa Leventis–worthy now?'

'Meaning…?'

'I felt like some matted poodle being dropped off at the groomer.'

'Mary,' he said, and she met his silvery eyes. 'I have said that you look beautiful on each occasion we've met.'

He had, she realised, but she looked quickly away, refusing to be mollified. It had been a long, lonely day but, worse than that, now he was here she was starting to remember why she'd said yes to this crazy charade…

In all her hurt and anger she had set aside his sheer assault to her senses and how divine he was. All the same, she would not be like Leo and the rest of Costa's minions and simply forgive him.

'Costa, what happened to your face?'

'I ran into a door.'

'Some door,' Mary retorted. 'Surely as your girl-friend I would know the truth?'

'No.'

'Your mother will want to know…'

'Perhaps, but she knows full well she'll get no answers.'

Costa let out a breath. He really did not want to tell Mary about being ambushed at Heathrow just after he'd left her, nor Eric Ridgemont's vile words about her.

Ridgemont he had taken care of one-handed.

Unfortunately, in his anger, he'd forgotten about the army Ridgemont travelled with.

'I had a slight accident after I left you. Afterwards I needed a new crown—preferably in time for the party—only your beloved NHS didn't want me to be concerned about that. They said I needed stitches, and also a scan.'

Mary watched him silently and he tried to turn it into a joke.

'I signed myself out and went private…' He took another sip of his drink before continuing 'And at my posh new hospital I got a scan and was stitched up, was woken every hour and a light shone in my eyes, so I signed myself out of there and went to a hotel. This morning I finally got my new crown…'

He showed her his new tooth amongst the row of lovely white ones and then, considering the conversation over, spread his gorgeous, slightly swollen mouth into a satisfied smile.

'I don't believe you, Costa—well, not about the door,' she said.

'Then don't.' Costa shrugged. 'We really need to go; the helicopter is waiting.'

'No.'

Mary shook her head. It was odd, but even in another country, and with no hint of a safety net, she was not scared to fall. And neither did she feel obligated to simply up and go just because of some cases beside her.

She had been here before, but she was older now.

The hardest part was behind her—she had walked out on Coral and lost her home and her job—and she suddenly felt liberated rather than scared…on the edge of something…or rather on the edge of *her*.

The old her.

The one who had been buried a long time ago and left unnoticed. Except it would seem she'd actually grown in that time, for it was a new Mary that had emerged.

'I'm not leaving here till we've sorted out our stories.'

Costa, though, had clearly grown a little too used to people jumping to his command. 'The helicopter is busy bringing in guests for tomorrow's party,' he said. 'It can't just sit idle while we play "getting to know you".'

'We can take the ferry, then.'

'I gave up taking the ferry a long time ago,' Costa scoffed.

But then he looked over and saw that Mary wasn't moving. In fact, Mary was more than happy to sit there all night.

'They're getting ready for something,' Mary commented, glancing around at the waiter, who had changed into evening attire. 'I think someone famous must be arriving…'

'The sun has brought them all out. They'll come off their yachts soon. Look at that,' he said, and she watched a family being moved to a table behind the rope. 'Making way for the oligarchs…'

'They're not moving us,' Mary said. 'Or rather, they're not moving you.'

'They would have once,' he assured her, and then she saw him realise that Mary had trapped him, and that they would be sitting here until they had all this sorted. 'You've changed,' he accused.

'I have,' Mary agreed. 'It must be the sun.'

'Well, whatever it is,' Costa begrudgingly admitted as he took out his phone, 'I like it.'

Stay cross, Mary told herself as he cancelled the helicopter. 'Can we start again?' Costa said and, turning off his phone, offered her his full attention. 'I hated that I couldn't be at the airport,' Costa said. 'Kristina was my last resort. Believe me, we do *not* get on.'

'Have you slept with her, then?'

'God, no!' He screwed up his nose. 'Why do you bring everything back to sex?'

'She hates you with too much passion, Costa, and she's also very beautiful.'

'Ice is beautiful—it doesn't mean I want to—' He halted what she was sure would be a crude response. 'Kristina hates everyone. I had to bribe her with a babymoon in Anapliró…'

'A babymoon?'

'An *extended* babymoon.' Costa rolled his eyes.

'Kristina should be a hostage negotiator rather than a PA, but she's hellishly efficient. And I got Leo out of bed before midday—which, believe me, is a miracle. He's angry with me too.'

Mary had been so hurt by his absence that she hadn't paused to think he might have actually had to jump through hoops in order to prevent her arriving alone and unmet. And while perhaps the realisation should have made her feel small, instead she suddenly felt looked-after, when she realised just how much worse this morning could have been.

'Thank you,' Mary said. 'I mean that.'

'No problem.' He glanced at all the cases. 'Clearly you and Leo got on!'

'He was lovely,' Mary nodded. She took a deep breath. 'So, let's get our stories straight.'

'Very well,' Costa said. 'What should I know about you?'

Mary swallowed. 'Costa, it's your family we're trying to fool. I don't have one.'

'I don't even know where you live,' he pointed out. 'Fine.' He let out a breath when he saw nothing was forthcoming. 'We'll just say London, but lately you've been spending a lot of time at mine.'

She watched him rack his brains, clearly trying to think what a true partner might already know just to get this settled.

'Are you gluten-intolerant?'

'What sort of question is that?'

'A lot of my dates are, and I'd have to let the kitchen know.'

'No, I'm not.' He made her dizzy, both indifferent and ardent, sometimes in the same sentence, at times just with his eyes... 'Costa, you bought me cake.'

'So I did.' He thought again. 'Any allergies?'

'None,' Mary said. 'Costa, we're not here to discuss me. I need to know more about *you*.'

He said nothing.

'Why don't we start with Roula?' she prompted, and then quoted Leo. 'Or rather, "poor Roula". I'm guessing she's the ex.'

'Leo talks too much.'

'How long were you together?'

'We were never together,' Costa said. 'We were promised as children. That's how it works over there...' He waved in the direction in which they would soon be heading.

'But you backed out?' Mary checked.

'No.'

'Costa, surely I'd know if I'm about to meet your parents...' she pointed out.

'There's just my mother,' Costa said. His face was tense, as if he'd realised that she really did need to know more. 'My father left when she got ill, and my mother ended up selling hot nuts from a caravan to make ends meet. The Kyrios family— Roula's family—decided I was no longer a suitable prospect.'

'Because your father left?' Mary frowned.

'That, and I guess they thought I might be like him and not a reliable provider...' He said it so blithely, so carelessly, that Mary was certain there was a whole lot more to it than that. Not that Costa would be sharing it.

'Roula married Dimitrios, a fisherman.'

'Oh.'

'You sound disappointed.'

'A bit,' she admitted. 'I was expecting a spurned lover.'

'Believe me, there are plenty of them—though not in Anapliró. I steer well away from any liaisons there. It would be the chapel at dawn...'

'Hence me?'

'Sort of.' Costa nodded, and then sighed. Because there was more, Mary was sure.

'What you need to know is that Roula's husband died in a boating accident a few years ago.'

'Ahh.'

'I could feel the eyes on me even at his funeral,' he admitted.

'Her eyes?'

'God, no. *We're* fine. More the older ones, who would like nothing more than to see us together.'

'Now that you're rich?'

'Of course.' He said it without malice, just stated it as fact. 'My mother too. Then there's Roula's family.'

'Yet they backed out?'

'They did,' Costa said. 'And because of that I got to be free and I built up the island. In fact, I employ most of them now. But it is not enough for them. There is… *Philotimo*.' He looked as if it could not easily be put into words as he tried to explain. 'It is something like honour. There are certain ways that I have long since let go. You know what families can be like.' He winced a little. 'I'm sorry, that was insensitive.'

'It's fine,' Mary said. 'I'm used to it. And,' she added, 'for the *temporary* record we're keeping, I love hearing about people's families.'

She would have liked to hear more, but Costa was reaching for his drink to drain it. At the same time she reached for him—just to halt him, just to get him to talk more… She didn't know. But although she'd remembered his beauty, she had forgotten the exquisite sensation of his skin brushing hers. It was a simple touch of their fingers, nothing more. As much contact as one might have if accepting change or taking a coat…yet it felt like so very much more.

Mary pulled back her hand, stunned that a mere brush of fingers could send volts of warmth through her, and more stunned that perhaps he had felt it too, for now he reclaimed her fingers across the table for the smallest of moments.

She did not recognise her own buffed nails, nor understand how she could be so mesmerised by the sight of her fingers wrapped gently in his.

* * *

He held her so gently, for he had seen them blanch at Ridgemont's touch and it had galled him more than he dared to consider.

What the hell was he doing? Costa wondered. She was just here to deliver him safe passage to freedom. So why did he want to simply sit in her presence and get to know her some more?

Costa decided he didn't.

He had sworn there would be no displays of affection without an audience, so he changed his touch to something else—a light pat, reassurance that the weekend would go okay—and his voice was a monotone as he glanced at the time.

'We'd better get on.'

'Of course.'

And, despite thinking he never would again, Costa Leventis found himself boarding the ferry to Anapliró.

CHAPTER SEVEN

COSTA DID NOT CARE for this method of transport.

It was a familiar passage, long since coded into his brain, and he loathed every lurch of the ferry. It was too chillingly familiar.

He sat on a metal bench beside Mary, who was turning to enjoy the beauty of Thira from a distance. In a while she would get her first glimpse of Anapliró, rising from the ocean.

Costa saw the retreat's helicopter flying overhead with his luggage, flown by a no doubt bemused pilot, wondering why his boss had chosen the ferry.

He'd stolen from his mother's purse to take the ferry alone that first time, determined to find his father and demand he return and face up to his responsibilities. He'd checked all the bars, asking if they'd seen Stavros Leventis…

He was aware suddenly of Mary's eyes on his face, checking out his stitches.

'Stop staring,' Costa said, but he turned and gave her a smile as he caught her out.

'You'd stare,' Mary said, 'if I'd arrived with a black eye and stitches.'

'True,' he conceded. 'Though I'd have left you back at the marina—that would have been too much to explain to Yolanda.'

She laughed. He did like to make her laugh.

'Are we going to meet her this evening?'

'We'll just drop in for a drink.' Costa nodded. 'She will be busy sorting things out for her party.'

'I got a book on basic Greek from the library...'

'Why? She speaks excellent English.'

'Yes, but she'll appreciate the effort.'

Costa frowned.

'If I was your real girlfriend I'd make the effort.'

'Ouáou!' Costa said, which was really just the equivalent of Mary's *Wow!* 'Would you really?'

'Of course.'

'That's terrifying!' Costa grinned as he said it, never quite sure if Mary was joking or not. 'But you honestly don't have to worry about speaking Greek. Most of our guests speak English and she converses well.'

'Leo said she's always busy,' Mary said, excited to get there. 'Why do you call her Yolanda?'

'She's the manager of the retreat. It would look odd if I had to say to a client that I need to check with my mother...'

She laughed again.

Costa did not.

The slow chug of the ferry and the lurch as it

started to turn reminded him too much of times best forgotten. He walked over to the rail, recalling half carrying, half dragging his mother up the ferry ramp the time she'd collapsed.

'I can't see, Costa.'

'I can,' he'd said, pleased that she couldn't see the look of sheer terror he'd been sure was on his face as he'd fought to keep his ten-year-old voice steady.

'I can't work if I can't see.'

'I can work.' His voice had cracked then, but it had already started to at times and it had been easy to blame it on his age. *'I look older...'*

He felt someone standing next to him.

'Such a view...' Mary sighed.

'Mary...'

He wanted to tell her as patiently as he could— explain that he did not require her to be his shadow, but now the slow, familiar turn of the ferry was in process and Costa knew that every last tourist would be coming to the rail soon.

'There she is.'

Mary followed his gaze, and it became clear that the *she* to which he referred was the island. Her first glimpse of Anapliró, rising from the ocean, was beyond words. It jutted out from the water in a daunting peak, and despite its lush green cover even Mary, with her untrained eye, could picture the lava that had created this rare treasure.

It was steep, and the houses carved into the hillside were dotted sparsely, except for one cluster of buildings.

'That's the village,' Costa said, then his hand guided her to look to the left. 'There is the retreat.'

'Where?' Mary stared, but then she saw it. It was so beautifully blended with the landscape that he'd had to point it out. Secluded for the most part by trees, it spread along the foreshore and into the hill beyond. 'It looks as if it's been there for ever.'

'Some of it almost has been,' Costa said.

Their approach added colour to the whitewashed buildings, and it made her breath hitch in her throat. There were bright blues and rusty oranges, and Costa showed her the landmarks, pointing first to a silver-domed church.

'That is where our guests who book the retreat for their wedding get married.'

It was stunning everywhere she looked, from the pools that were like sapphires slotted into the hillside, to the stunning ocean and the yachts in the bay.

'I lived there growing up,' Costa said, pointing to a stretch of harbour, clearly having decided it was something she perhaps ought to know. Then he moved his hand and pointed higher. 'My grandparents had a home in the hills. My mother lived there till my *yaya* died;

now she has her own residence in the grounds of the retreat.'

'How...?' Mary asked, utterly bewildered, for the island was breathtakingly beautiful. She was speechless at the thought of a poor boy from the village achieving all this. 'How did you do it?'

'That is not up for discussion.'

'With me?'

'With anyone,' Costa countered. 'I don't share my life with anyone, Mary.' He clearly meant it, but he added, 'I was born under a lucky star.'

'Oh, please...'

He sighed. 'Nemo is here to collect us, so I should...' He slipped an arm around her shoulders. 'He's Roula's brother.'

'How did he know we'd be on-board?'

'The helicopter pilot, I guess. I told you—everyone knows everyone else's business here.' He turned her to face him then. 'So, before we dock, tell me more about you.'

'Like what? I'm really very boring.'

'Okay,' Costa said. 'I'll tell people that, shall I, when they ask about you? "She's really very boring." I don't think so.'

'My star sign is Aries.'

'Yes, because it was your birthday last week. Come on, Mary, give me something here. What would a lover know about Mary Jones?'

'Perhaps you should have attached a questionnaire to the contract,' Mary said, knowing full well he had chosen this moment when she was held in his arms to ask her these things. 'Costa, you're paying me to hang off your arm and be kissed on demand.'

'Didn't they teach you in escort school not to constantly remind the guy that he's paying for it? Because it really doesn't help, Mary.'

Costa took a breath, as if suddenly he loathed the charade that they'd created. Whether he wanted to or not, he cared far too much about Mary, and had done since the very first night.

Mary sighed, as she'd thought of something she had better let him know. 'I didn't go to "escort school", as you call it. The fact is—'

'I apologise,' he cut in. 'That was crass of me.'

'No, Costa…'

'Let's just drop it,' he suggested. 'It's probably best that I kiss you now, if that's okay.'

'For the sake of our audience?'

'Of course.'

His kiss was different this time, just his mouth moving over hers and his hands on her hips as if placed by a director.

Except the director had forgotten to direct the placement of Mary's…

'Don't stand there like you're sleeping on your feet,' Costa reminded her as he moved his mouth back a fraction.

Mary wasn't sleeping. In fact, she might very easily weep at the taste of this passionate man's plastic kiss.

'There,' he said, and drew his head back. He looked at her with no trace of affection. 'That should do.'

If there had been a napkin handy, she was rather sure he'd have wiped it over his mouth.

CHAPTER EIGHT

'WON'T BE LONG NOW,' Costa said as they sat holding hands in the back of a luxurious car. But there were no toying fingers; there was no press of thumbs.

Mary glanced up and saw that Nemo was watching her in the rear-view mirror. He had dark brown eyes that were not awkward when they met hers; they were just…brown.

'It's quite a drive,' Mary ventured to Costa as the car hugged the coastal road at speed, making her catch her breath at times. 'Well, you'd be used to it, I guess…'

'Not really. I generally fly in.'

They passed some gorgeous old houses, and Costa perked up. He pointed to the hills ahead and told her about a new restaurant. 'Apparently it's amazing,' Costa said. 'My head chef and the restaurateur are rivals…'

'Really?'

'So I am duty bound to take you there to check out the competition. We'll try and go before we leave.'

He moved a strand of her hair and kissed her cheek and she turned to him so readily.

Too readily.

'I can't wait,' Mary said, and lightly kissed him back, as if it was the most natural thing in the world to do.

The trouble for Mary, though, was that it was beginning to feel like that.

'Enough now,' he said into the shell of her ear, then pulled back.

Damn!

Of course—the sudden affection and sweet talk had been for the benefit of Nemo.

Stung, she pulled away as they swung into a long driveway. She saw the retreat, low and vast and like a hidden temple...

'I thought...'

She was silent then, for she had assumed it had been built from scratch, or something, but it really was as if it had stood there for ever. Only now wasn't the time for questions. Actually, asking questions wasn't her place in this situation—but it was like playing catch-up on a treasure hunt and knowing you were missing so many important clues.

'Thank you,' Costa said, as a bellboy brought their luggage into a villa, carrying it through to the main bedroom. She glimpsed a vast bed draped in dark navy and ached to peer in, but she stood there, a stranger in Costa's home—or rather, his Anapliró residence, for she could see it was not a *home*.

'It's incredible,' Mary said, when the bellboy had gone.

It truly was, for the stone walls should make it feel cold, yet the one wall of glass doors which could clearly be opened up to the outside captured the low sun and the view was enticing.

It was certainly a male space, Mary thought as she walked around, avoiding the subject of the bedroom. She looked up at the high ceiling and then to the gorgeous rugs scattered on the floor, taking in what was to be her home for the next couple of nights.

Mary was used to new homes—or at least she had been while growing up. Used to being the new girl in strange surroundings and always trying to get a feel for a new place. This entire space was clearly stamped as his.

'Here.' Costa was clearly not avoiding the subject, and opened up a white door to direct her into a guest room.

Or rather a guest *suite*, with a bed dressed in white linen and a beautiful stone-tiled bathroom. For this weekend it would all be hers…and yet it was the dark navy bed in his room that still burned her eyes.

'You have your own pool, though it's too small for swimming…'

He walked across the room to open up some

French doors and there was the sound of cascading water. As she peered out she could see that she had her own dip pool and fountain, like a mini oasis.

'You can call the restaurant or the spa if you want food, or a massage or whatever...' He nodded to the bedside phone. 'For anything you want, really.'

'Press two for Costa?'

'Sorry...' He gave her a smile. 'It's not wired into my room. As I said, you have to come to me.'

She wandered into the kitchen and opened up a vast fridge, looking at the choice of food and wine. Then she peered back into the master bedroom, where her luggage had been placed, but deliberately didn't go in. She just stared from the double doors. Her heart was thumping in her chest, and the real dilemma she had been trying to ignore was rising.

This wasn't real. She had to constantly remind herself that the sole reason she was here was because, come Monday, she would have the money to move on and get her chance for a fresh start.

She had made lists all week, added up the pros and the cons—just as if this was a job offer.

And it was.

There was one point she had failed to add, though it belonged in both columns, being both a pro and a con.

Mary liked him.

No, it was more than that. Mary was just a little bit crazy about Costa Leventis.

Even when he hadn't been able to get to the airport himself that morning, still he'd sent someone, and the efforts he had gone to meant more than he could possibly know.

And although they bickered, for Mary it felt like freedom—because he allowed her to be herself.

Whoever Mary Jones was.

As Costa made a phone call she looked again at her gorgeous new luggage, all waiting to be un-packed—but where?

'Hey…' He came to stand beside her, the door-way so wide that they didn't even touch. 'Do you want someone to come and unpack your things?' he offered.

'No, thank you.'

'Then I'm going to have a swim.'

He moved past her, stripping off his shirt. Then, as he unclipped his case, she saw the dark bruises on his ribs and just couldn't stop herself.

She said it again. 'Some door!'

'Yeah, some door,' he said, unbuckling his belt.

Really, she knew she should take her cue and go, but she honestly thought he was about to elabo-rate…to explain things. Honestly thought that now they were properly alone there would be a chance to talk, to get to know each other.

But instead he stripped off.

Just like that.

She stood in the doorway and watched as Costa Leventis got naked.

'Costa!'

'What?' He turned and saw her still standing there. 'You're the one standing there watching me.'

He pulled on some swimwear, but not fast enough for Mary to avoid seeing a full-frontal naked glimpse of Costa.

He was stunning. She'd guessed he'd be toned, but although large, he was trim too. And hairy! She'd listened to the women chatting in the salon as they breezed through magazines, and of course she'd read them too, before recycling them—even the sealed section that had come in one. Well, she'd actually saved that particular magazine…

But this was no glossy two-dimensional image that danced in her mind. And though his muscular legs and long, strong arms had not escaped her attention, nor the fan of hair on his chest and that black snaky line downwards, it was the other bit that was now permanently fixed in her brain. Mary had never seen a naked man before. That…that part of him had been lifting, sort of moving independently of him, and even though it was covered now, as he walked past her, it was as if she could still see it.

'Are you coming for a swim?' he asked.

'Aren't we supposed to be going to your mother's?'

'It's not a doctor's appointment. Anyway, if we *were* real…' he gestured to the bed '…she'd expect me to be late.'

He left her standing there and she just stared at the bed.

If they were a real couple, Costa and Mary would be tumbling on it.

She was jealous of them, the other Mary and Costa.

Jealous of him and his ease with himself.

She wished she could just strip off on a whim while carrying on a conversation with a virtual stranger.

Of course she should move her things to the guest room now and that would be that—for she was hardly going to come knocking at his door demanding sex!

She walked over to the bed and ran a light hand over the velvety fabric. And found she desperately wanted him.

She recalled his words: *There are safer ways to chase adventure.* For Mary, Costa was both safe and an adventure. So she did not unpack, nor move her cases. She just opened one, selected a little amber bikini and changed into it—though not with the same ease Costa had demonstrated.

She was burning from the roots of her hair to her freshly painted toes, still a little stunned at the sight of a naked Costa, as she stepped out into an evening that was darkening towards night, where only the pool was gently lit and Costa was swimming in it.

She sat on the edge and dipped first her toes and then her legs in. The water was tepid, and bliss on her skin after a long angst-filled day. From there she watched him, slicing through the water, turning at each end. Clearly he'd meant it when he'd said he was going for a swim.

He came up beside her a good while later and leant his arms on the edge, a little breathless and clearly in a better mood.

'Aren't you going to get in?' he asked.

'No.' She shook her head. 'I'll just sit.'

'It's deep and the water is perfect.'

'I can't swim,' she admitted. 'There—you've got something for your list. Mary can't swim.'

'Seriously?' He looked a bit stunned by the fact. 'Don't they teach you at school in England?'

'They do.' She nodded. 'But I got banned on my first lesson.'

'For…?' Costa asked.

Such a simple question. He could never know the hurt behind her answer, for it had happened the day her mother died.

'I escaped from my class and went over to the diving pool.' She could actually see herself, climbing the endless ladder, her little legs determined rather than shaking, knowing she had to hurry before she got caught. 'I dived off the top board…'

'Go, Mary!' He laughed. 'The top one?'

'Yes.' She nodded and looked to see that he was smiling up at her. 'I didn't think it through, of course, and I had to be rescued. Then my mother had to come and collect me…'

'You had her then?' Costa enquired gently.

'I did,' Mary said, 'though not for much longer.'

It was as if the pool was a magic lantern now, flashing forgotten images into a sky full of stars.

'My mother told me there'd be no treats for a week, but she didn't really mean it, and my dad—' She stopped.

'Your dad?'

'Mr Sensible…' Mary attempted, using the teasing term that she and her granny had reserved for him. '"Mary needs to learn…"' she quoted, but then she stopped again, for in this quiet space, under a darkening Anapliró sky, with Costa patiently waiting, she finally dared to look that time in the face.

Mary could see the worry in her father's features that night, feel his hands taking hers as he suggested to her mother that they not go out. He'd known, despite her defiant, sullen stance, just how upset she was.

Not that she shared that small revelation with Costa.

'The school were furious; they banned me from swimming lessons for the entire term.'

'So they refused to teach you the one thing that might have saved you?'

'I guess… Anyway, it didn't matter. I changed schools soon after that.' She looked down at him. 'Who taught you?'

'I don't know.' Costa shrugged. 'I just swam…'

She frowned. 'Galen and I used to swim in the sea each morning, further out each time.'

'Galen's your friend?' she checked, for she'd heard Kristina say his name.

'Not really a friend. We were at school together for a while, and then in the military. Now we share an office building and I'm constantly being warned not to borrow his miserable PA...'

'Sounds like a friend to me.'

'Maybe,' he agreed. 'We used to call him *rompót* at school—robot.'

'That's so mean.'

'No, it was a compliment. He's brilliant—like, seriously so.' He smiled then. 'Very serious. He's why I can't fly you on a private jet...'

'And I thought you were principled?'

'Nope.'

She thought he was about to haul himself out, but then he noticed her eyes on the water, as if he saw her longing to get in.

'No diving allowed,' he teased and offered his hand.

There was absolutely no ulterior motive behind it, she told herself. To Costa the pool was for swimming, and it was clear he found the water relaxing.

So Mary accepted the invitation and took his hand and dropped in, feeling the embrace of the water and the steadiness of his hand as she searched for the bottom.

'Should we move to the shallow end?' Mary

asked, because while Costa appeared to be standing, she could not feel the floor.

'There isn't one,' he told her. 'This would have been a *frigidarium*. People would come here after their time in the warmer pools.'

'It's warm, though...'

'We're not in Ancient Greece now.'

Still holding his hand, she took a breath and submerged herself, and came up to see his smile.

'If you want, I can teach you to swim.'

She gave a slightly mocking laugh, for she was *so* not falling for that, but Costa did not return it.

'I told you the night we met. I don't do double speak.'

Mary rather wished he did, though, as he placed her hands back on the stone edge. She wished *his* hands could be on her, and that they might linger and events might unfold. Yet Costa had told her it was for her to make such a move.

'Stretch out on your front...just get used to the water,' he told her, as he did the same, and she clung on to the edge with both hands, slowly getting used to the weightlessness of the water. 'My office is in Kolonaki in Athens,' he said, and then he began to tell her more of what she might need to know—that his office looked over an ancient square, that his apartment was a drive away and overlooked the ocean. 'I swim every morning. You'd know that.'

He gave her a smile as they lay on their fronts and she turned to him. 'And I don't join you?' Mary smiled.

Not yet, Costa was about to say, but instead he looked away. Even if it was the type of thing he might say when they were playing their parts, there was no room for blurred lines here.

They lay on their fronts, holding the stone edge, not touching, just floating, as the worries of the world dispersed into the mineral-rich water.

'How did your boss take it?' he asked.

'As expected,' Mary responded. 'She fired me.'

But then, as always, Mary surprised him. Because she suddenly smiled and kicked her legs.

'It was actually liberating.'

'Good,' Costa said, liking her smile.

'I headed to the airport hotel and ate all the chocolate in the minibar and then the nuts,' she informed him. She'd felt guilty about it at the time, but not now. 'And then I turned on a movie and lay on the bed and said *gia parti mou*…'

'Good for you,' Costa told her.

They floated on, the water holding them apart and then drifting them together occasionally, so that their shoulders brushed or their arms touched. She wondered why she did not feel shy, and why she could be nearly naked beside him yet feel soothed. Suspended rather than adrift.

But then the outside lights came on, and Costa sighed at the reminder of the time and where they needed to be.

'Ought we to go?' Mary asked, knowing this little interlude was over.

'Yes.'

She could hear the reluctance in his response.

'Why do you hate coming here?' Mary asked as they faced each other in the water. Now she looked not at the stitches, nor at the bruises, just at him.

Costa didn't quite know how to answer. Right now he did not hate being home. He could hear the *grylos* starting to chirp, and the sounds of laughter in the distance, could smell the scent of the ocean beyond.

He didn't answer her question, but it didn't matter now. Because their arms were touching and their hips were lightly bumping together,

'Why did you kiss me like a mannequin on the ferry?' she asked.

'I don't like performing for an audience,' Costa said, and took her hand to help guide her out.

But it was Mary who moved in closer and kissed him—perhaps because she had to, perhaps because she had the safety of knowing a kiss was all it could be for now, for there were places this seemingly happy couple needed to be.

The horrors of the day dissolved as he reached for her waist and glided her closer.

They kissed lightly, but slowly. Not a practice kiss now, nor one for the benefit of others. Just two adults finally alone. He pulled her to face him, and Mary cared not that her feet would not reach the ground, for she was held right against him.

His tongue was thorough, and it seemed to inspire her to wrap her legs around him. She didn't know what she was doing, except that it felt like perfection. His hands were holding her waist and she coiled her arms around his neck and just sank into his kiss as his hands roamed the sides of her body.

Mary felt as she had at the bar that night, burning and taut, only now there was the warm thrill of his bare skin beneath her thighs.

It was Costa who pulled back, for with Mary he would take his time.

'Still beautiful,' he said as he pulled his head back and looked at her spiky lashes, with her hips still in his hands.

'I don't want the guest room tonight,' Mary confessed.

'Thank God for that.' He smiled.

Costa knew he would wait for tonight, but as he stroked one nipple to a peak through her bikini top he heard her low moan. She wrapped herself more tightly around him and he removed the top entirely. A quick climax for Mary would be his absolute pleasure right now…

Costa lifted her a bit and she closed her eyes as he tasted her breast. It felt as if he was stirring her deep inside with each slow suck. And when she forgot to breathe he gave her a brief pause before moving his mouth to the other one.

He moaned, and it shivered through her, and then he kissed her, more deeply this time, and drew her more tightly against him. His hardness pressed against her heat, and after a day that had felt so fraught, she felt so very free.

His hands were on her breasts now as she clung on, stroking them and pinching them as her body sourced the centre of him…

Bed now, Costa was thinking, for there was protection there. Except right now she was warm against him, and nearly there, pressed into him. So he positioned her on the tip of his erection and enjoyed the humming noise she made, her obvious pleasure…

Such pleasure…

She had thought it would be complicated, but it was definitely not, for as he undid the ties on the bottoms of her bikini all she felt was relief, as if finally discarding some impossible weight.

'Costa…' She was on the very edge of something new and delicious, and yet there was not a shred of fear.

'Don't you dare fake it…' he warned, and she did not know what he could possibly mean, because she was on fire in the tepid water.

'Take me to bed,' she begged, for she was desperate.

There was no time for bed, though. Costa was burning to feel her come on him—just that and no more.

He stripped off with the same ease he had in the bedroom. More ease perhaps.

Mary was so focussed on pleasure that he saw it took a second for her mired brain to register the splash as his swimwear hit the stone tiles at the edge of the pool.

'There…' she moaned, as if he didn't know that the pearl he stroked was unravelling her.

She was tense in his arms because she did not know how to deal with the frenzy he was firing up inside her. The first probing of his fingers had her biting down on his shoulder in both shock and bliss.

The turn-on of Mary being a little bit savage brought him to the brink. Her short rapid breaths, the tension in her body, the feel of her on the edge, rendered him suddenly more selfish, and now this climax was no longer just for one, but for two.

Her hand had found him beneath the water, and

he groaned at her light touch, and at the agony of the tease as she removed her hand.

'Mary...'

Costa said something throaty in Greek and lifted her. The first nudge of him hurt, only it wasn't the size of him that stopped her. It was the warm velvet skin she had felt with her hand. And there was one single thing she knew about sex: he was unprotected.

'What...?' He must have felt her tense, and he pulled back to see her pained features. 'What's wrong?'

'Costa...' She didn't know how to tell him, how to find the words to express what she wanted to say. 'You said just a swim...'

He closed his eyes and almost dropped all contact, except they were out of *her* depth, not his, so he moved her to the edge, then hauled himself out.

Mary tried not to look at his naked arousal, but failed, and then he was already back inside the villa.

Like riled flatmates they took turns with the bathroom and dressed behind closed doors.

In fact, Mary used a bidet for the first time in her life, just to cool the burn that his first nudge had caused. She wondered if she could get away with not telling him she was a virgin.

Because after that brief glimpse of heaven Mary definitely no longer wanted to be!

She was certain that she wanted her first to be him. Mary could think no further ahead than that.

'Ready?' Costa asked as she came out of the bedroom, dressed in the mint-green dress, this time with her damp hair tied back—not that he would notice, because he barely looked in her direction.

'Yes,' she said, picking up her bag and taking out the card she'd bought.

'What's this?' he asked.

Mary glanced up and tried to face him for the first time since…

He looked stunning, of course, in pale linen trousers and a fine-knit top that showed off the toned body around which she'd so recently been coiled. His black hair was wet and brushed back and he looked as thoroughly disgruntled as she herself felt. Well, not disgruntled…but she felt all knotted up inside.

'A birthday card.'

It was a very nice card, Mary thought, with '50' written in gold as well as a pair of false eyelashes stuck to the front, which Yolanda could peel off and wear if she so chose.

'It's funny.'

'I don't do cards.'

'Well, I do,' she said, but he'd already stalked off. 'Costa,' she called as she caught up with him and they passed the pool where their wet swimwear still lay. 'About before…'

'Not now,' he clipped. 'Let's get this over with.'

The retreat was gently lit and they walked along

a softly lit path an arm's length apart, past the occasional villa and the restaurant. There was a herby scent in the air, and the chirrup of crickets matched the rub between her legs.

'The crickets are loud.'

'Grylo,' Costa snapped back. 'I hate them.'

'I like them…'

The air was thick—not just with the scent of herbs and the sound of *grylo,* but with a tension Mary found most unfamiliar: the hum of unsated desire.

'Costa,' she said, 'can we discuss before?'

'Let's just get through Yolanda's interrogation, shall we?'

'Costa, please…'

'There's nothing we need to discuss—and anyway, we're here…'

But although she could see they were at the gates, there was so much to discuss.

'I thought it was mutual,' Costa said.

'And it was. I was enjoying it…'

'I don't need the ego-stroke, Mary. Save it for your clients.'

'There are no clients,' Mary retorted. 'There never have been.'

'What?'

'I'm a virgin…'

He just stood there and looked at her in silence for a very long time. And then in the distance his name was called—presumably by his mother.

'Costa!'

Yet he didn't answer her. Instead, he had some questions for Mary. Oh, yes, he did.

'So what the hell was that back at the pool?' Costa checked. 'You came on to me. And I know that for a fact, because I wanted to be very sure it was something you wanted.'

'And I did.'

'So when were you going to tell me you're a virgin?'

'Does it matter?'

'Of course it damn well matters,' Costa snapped, and then cursed in Greek. 'I paid for an escort. I paid for a no-strings weekend to make my life less complicated, not more!'

Yolanda could clearly wait no longer, for the gates had parted and there they were, lit by security lights and facing each other in the middle of a storm of words.

'Jesus!' he hissed. 'You really know how to pick your moments, don't you, Mary?'

Mary turned and looked beyond the gates, to where there was a vast pool and several people setting up for the party tomorrow. But it was Yolanda who drew the eye, for she was possibly the most glamorous woman Mary had ever seen.

Waving them in from her electric wheelchair while sipping a drink, she wore a cerise smile along with a turquoise caftan, and her hair was the most stunning chocolate-brown with gold highlights. She was absolutely as beautiful as her son.

'*Kalimera.*' Mary smiled.

'It's *kalispera*,' Costa corrected—not that his mother noticed.

'What happened to your eye?' she exclaimed when she saw Costa's cuts and bruises.

'A door.'

'Oh, please,' she said as she hugged him. But just as Costa had predicted, she didn't delve. 'It's so good you're here; it's been far too long. A year, at least…'

'Don't give her your sympathy vote.' Costa was clearly more than used to playing a part and he smiled as he glanced over to Mary. 'She omits to mention we had lunch in Athens two weeks ago.'

Yolanda laughed, and her gaze turned to where Mary stood.

She wasn't even feeling awkward now—just sad to receive his fake smile the same way she had received his fake kiss on the ferry.

'So, this is Mary…' Yolanda looked her up and down. 'I'm sorry, I missed your full name…'

'Stop fishing,' Costa warned her lightly as they made their way over to a gorgeous covered veranda away from the pool. He pulled out a chair for Mary, who took a seat as she answered Yolanda's question.

'Mary Jones.'

'Welcome, Mary.'

She went to pour Mary a small glass of the liquor she was drinking—the same thing Costa had been drinking at the marina, she thought. Though still oddly tempted to try it, Mary politely declined. 'No, thank you…'

'To welcome you,' Yolanda insisted, adding water to her own.

It was Costa who sorted it out. 'Mary doesn't drink.'

'At all?' Yolanda checked. 'It's just ouzo…'

'There's no *just* ouzo. I'd have to carry her back to the villa,' Costa quipped, and added water to his own little glass.

'Have the two of you eaten?' Yolanda asked.

'No, but we're not staying…'

'Costa,' Yolanda moaned, 'surely we can have dinner together…?'

'And we often do…'

'Not here, though.'

'And not tonight.' He changed the subject. 'Are you ready for tomorrow?'

'I think so.'

Yolanda nodded and, though she spoke directly to her son, Mary could feel that her gaze kept drifting towards her. She was clearly wary of the outsider.

'I wish I'd listened to you and just hosted a dinner in Athens,' his mother said.

'I warned you.'

'You did.'

She spoke more about the upcoming party. The lights, the drinks, the people who were coming… And Costa attempted to carry on the conversation as he tried to work out the enigma called Mary who sat beside him as his mother chatted on.

Mary's pained features in the pool were flashing in his mind. Had he hurt her? Wrongly assumed they had been driven by mutual desire? And what the hell was she playing at?

'Are you listening, Costa…?'

Yolanda pulled him back to her party issues.

'Nemo is sulking because of course I need him to work tomorrow. He's head of security,' she explained to Mary, 'so I need him on duty. Honestly, the trouble of mixing business and pleasure.'

'Indeed,' Costa said, and hoped Mary knew that one was aimed at her.

'Can you speak to him, please?' Yolanda said. 'He should be doing his checks soon.'

'Sure.'

'And then there's poor Roula…' Yolanda continued, and looked over to Mary. 'I'm so sorry to bring her up in front of you, but better out than in—especially with my party tomorrow…'

'It's fine.' Mary smiled, clearly rather grateful that Costa had given her a heads-up on that.

'She is so low at the moment, Costa. She smiles and laughs, but I can tell there is something troubling her.'

'Am I to speak to her too?' Costa checked, tongue firmly in cheek. 'Should we set up a little counselling tent for me at your party, so any disgruntled staff can drop in?'

'Costa!' Yolanda laughed at the very idea, but then she looked serious. 'I'm sure it's not a work issue.'

'Then it has nothing to do with me.'

'I'm not so sure…'

'We never even dated,' Costa snapped. 'We were kids when you all cooked up our future.' He was so fed up with hearing it, and also annoyed at his mother for her lack of tact. 'And what the hell are you doing bringing it up now?'

'Costa…'

It was a quiet warning. Only it wasn't his mother who'd warned him he'd gone too far. Instead, it was quiet little Mary Jones from London! What had happened to her hanging off his arm and being kissed on demand?

He shot her a look to remind her of her role.

Mary didn't see it; she was digging in her bag and trying to resume niceties. 'I got this for you, Yolanda…'

She handed over the first ever bottle of perfume she had bought, blushing at the clearly last-minute nature of her gift, but glad it had come beautifully wrapped.

'But it's not my birthday until Sunday.'

'I know. This is just to thank you for welcoming me.'

'Mary!' Yolanda beamed as she opened it, and then squirted it in the air and inhaled. 'I love it!'

She squirted it on her neck and her wrists, and then jokingly on a clearly sulking Costa, who rolled his eyes but, obviously used to his mother's ways, just put up with it.

'See what Mary got for me.'

She turned eyes like silver headlamps to Mary then, and looked at her properly for the first time. She and Costa had the same stunning eyes—in colour only, though. Yolanda's were far less guarded and, unlike Costa's, Yolanda's eyes, though suspicious, were open-hearted.

'Enough about Roula. Costa is right—how rude of me to bring her up in front of you. So, Mary, how long have you been dating my son?'

'A couple of months.' She smiled and hoped she'd got that part right.

'And have your parents met him, or am I the first?'

She looked from Mary to Costa, who had given her a little tap, only Yolanda didn't take the subtle hint.

'What's wrong with asking that?'

'Mary lost her parents.'

'Oh, no!' Yolanda said, and such was the distress in her voice that Mary loathed every single one of her lies.

Suddenly the events of this morning, the disaster of the pool, her admission to Costa all caught up with her. She could feel the undeserved balm of his mother's concern and was appalled to realise she was about to cry.

And, worse, Yolanda clearly saw that she was.

'I come to you.'

Yolanda started to haul herself out of her wheelchair to give Mary what might be a very dangerous hug—for if Yolanda so much as touched her then she thought she might completely unravel.

Costa intervened. 'Leave her,' he warned, while privately wondering what the hell had happened to his life.

His mother, who usually offered the evil eye along with a smile to anyone who wasn't Roula, was actually bonding with his escort—who, as it turned out, was a virgin and about to break down and cry…

Had he hurt her?

'You can be so cold,' Yolanda chided her son as she sat back down.

Thank goodness for Costa, Mary thought, for he'd given her a moment to regroup and collect herself as Yolanda moved the topic to what she clearly hoped would be more cheerful things.

'So, how did you meet?' Yolanda asked. 'He tells me nothing.'

'Online,' Costa said.

'No, we didn't!' Mary exclaimed, assuming he was lightening things with a tease. 'I was seeing a mutual friend, and I guess we just…' She looked over to Costa and his expression was like thunder, although he did cover for her.

'Mary was miserable with him and I pointed it out.'

'As you tend to,' Yolanda said. 'Wait there. I have something I need you two to try.'

As Yolanda disappeared into her villa, Costa felt Mary shoot him a look.

'What was that about?' she demanded. 'We agreed—'

'That was before.' Costa met her glare and, still reeling from her revelation, didn't have the energy to lie. 'The "slight accident" I had? With the "door"? It was a fight. With Ridgemont. Well, with his security team, really.'

Mary frowned. 'About the Middle East deal?'

'No!' He screwed closed his eyes to stop his eyeballs popping out and his stitches snapping. 'What do you *think* it was about? It was poor form of me, apparently, to leave with his date.'

'I never asked you to fight.'

'I would have defended any woman spoken about like that,' Costa said tartly.

Though perhaps not with his fists. He had thought those days long gone.

'Let's just smile through her baclava. I hate the stuff!'

Sure enough, Yolanda was back with a tray. 'My secret recipe,' she told Mary. 'I am making more tomorrow...'

'What's the point of getting a party catered,' Costa asked, 'if you're going to spend the day cooking?'

'Everyone loves my baclava.' She gave him a slice and then cut one for Mary.

'Try it.'

'Yes, please!' Mary said. She guessed that Costa's new crown might not be quite ready to be bathed in honey, so she dived in as he mashed up the little bit that was on his plate. 'Wow!' she said, and she was not exaggerating. 'That is...'

'Costa?' Yolanda asked.

'It's good,' he said, having taken not a bite. 'Oh, look. There's Nemo now. I'll go and have a word with him.'

It actually wasn't awkward to be left alone with Yolanda. Costa's mother didn't push, and she didn't try to prise out information—at least not at first. In fact she just sat for a moment, as Mary ate her own baclava along with Costa's.

But then Yolanda let out a long breath and admitted her doubts about the party. 'Parties are hard work. Especially your own.'

'Can I help with anything?'

'Aside from a day of cooking, it's all done,' Yolanda said. 'At least I hope so. I just want everyone to have fun. No speeches and all that stuff...' She waved the thought away with her hand.

But then she did ask a question.

'What happened to Costa's face? And please don't tell me a door. *Éla*,' she said, and swiftly translated, 'Come, now...'

'He told me a door too,' Mary said.

'I shouldn't worry, really,' Yolanda sighed. 'Costa always comes out on top. Whatever he puts his mind to, he gets. When we had no money he always made sure I had a doctor and medicine...' She looked out to the beautiful surroundings. 'He transformed Anapliró, though God knows how...'

She looked over and Mary honestly didn't know what to say. She didn't know how the other Mary, the one who was allowed to love him, might have responded.

'I tell you,' Yolanda continued, 'that boy was born under—'

'He's worked hard to get where he is,' Mary cut in.

She was a little tired of hearing about Costa and his lucky star, or his Midas touch, or condescending sniffs like Ridgemont's about 'new money'. From all she could see, he hadn't just snapped his fingers and transformed the island—he'd worked hard for it.

Except she was taking it out on the wrong person, Mary realised, when she saw Yolanda's wide eyes. 'Sorry.'

God, she really was the worst paid date in the world, Mary thought, because now she was snapping at his mother.

When Costa came back, Mary asked where the bathroom was—not just to be polite and give them time together, but also to hide her burning face for a moment. She should have just smiled and nodded at Yolanda and stayed the hell out of it…

As he would have wanted.

Mary stayed in the bathroom for ages. She didn't even care if they thought she had an upset stomach or something. She just sat with her head in her hands, trying to fathom how to face Costa alone.

This was work, she reminded herself, just as a night spent folding pink towels in the salon had been…

Except this was a job she loved.

CHAPTER NINE

THEIR WALK BACK via the beach was beautiful. The sand was warm beneath her feet and the gentle lap of water was soothing. There was a massive moon over the water, on the very edge of being full, and it should have been perfect.

It almost was.

'It looks like a big ball of white chocolate,' Mary said into the silence as he walked alongside her. 'Well, like it's been licked at one of the edges a bit.'

He didn't laugh, or do anything really—just walked in silence. Maybe he was waiting for an explanation. Or maybe he was just killing time, Mary thought. Getting through the long-dreaded weekend.

'Do you think she believed us?' Mary asked.

'What?'

'Yolanda—do you think she believed us?'

'You really know how to play smoke and mirrors, don't you?' he accused. 'Hey, let's focus on the most irrelevant detail, why don't we?'

'The party is the reason I'm here.' Mary's voice

was starting to rise, and she wasn't used to the sound of it doing that. 'And if we're going to sort something out by tomorrow then—'

'There *is* no tomorrow.'

'We *can* sort it out,' she insisted. 'Talk it through.'

'Talk what through?'

'I just need to know what you're thinking.'

'Mary, you're asking me to talk to you, to tell you what I'm thinking. You want to discuss this as if it were some sort of relationship in need of rescue, when it's absolutely not. The only thing I need to know is, did I hurt you?'

'No.'

'Was I too rough?'

'You weren't rough,' Mary said. 'If you'd known the truth you'd have taken things slower, but it was actually *very* nice…'

'If I'd known,' Costa responded tartly, ignoring the last part, 'then, believe me, you wouldn't be here.'

'Oh, so you'd prefer a more experienced date?'

'Why are you here, Mary?' He turned and bluntly asked her. 'Money?'

She nodded.

'Anything else?'

'A weekend of sun and a party.'

'And?'

'Sex.'

'I made it very clear I was hiring you to act as

my girlfriend. Brilliant acting skills, by the way—the perfume, learning some Greek…'

'I took it seriously,' Mary answered primly, trying to hide the little alarms that were being triggered as he approached her landmine zones. She'd actually been herself—and he'd clearly loathed it. 'Method acting, I think they call it. I got a book once from—'

'The library?' he finished for her.

'I'm sorry if I misled you.'

'*Misled?* You're a liar, Mary,' he told her, 'and a very good one. And that is entirely your prerogative. I'm not judging you. I've lied to get ahead too. But may I suggest you don't attempt no-strings sex when you have no idea what's involved?'

'I wanted no-strings sex, though.' She heard his angry hiss. 'I honestly did. I like how you make me feel and I wanted a weekend of fun and a party and making love…'

'Let's stop right there. Because not only do I not "make love", but in the middle of the no-strings sex you say you want, clearly you changed your mind.'

She was silent.

'You knew you were out of your depth.'

'No.'

'Yes,' he insisted. 'I *was* in the pool with you, Mary…'

'The reason I stopped you wasn't because I was scared, or regretting things, or faking it, or worried that it might hurt—well, maybe a bit…' She took a breath. 'I don't know how to say this.'

'Go ahead!'

'Well, I wasn't…' She stopped herself again.

'Please,' he invited, 'let's just have it out here and now.'

'I wasn't going to stake my sexual health on a slut like you!'

There—she'd said it. In fact, she'd shouted it. And for the first time in almost for ever she'd let her temper out.

'God help me…' Costa muttered, because she was the most confusing person ever placed on this earth!

'I've known from the start that we're not going anywhere,' Mary said. 'I accept that.'

'Oh, you *accept* that, do you? Mary, it was never even up for negotiation.'

He wasn't just angry with her, but with himself too—because he'd have had her in the pool and they both knew it. And he never had unprotected sex. *Never.*

'Are you even on the Pill?'

'I started it the night you left.'

Costa gave a black laugh, but then changed it to a somewhat incredulous smile. 'I admire you, Mary,' he said, only he knew he didn't sound particularly complimentary. 'When you go for something, you really go for it, don't you?'

'Perhaps...'

'Perhaps?' He turned in simple amazement at her complete understatement. 'Diving off the top board, a birthday night out with a brute, a weekend in Greece as an escort when you've never even—'

He stopped, because he could not focus on her innocence; it was much easier to allow his natural suspicion to take over than to indulge in dangerous thoughts about the intoxicating woman in front of him.

His eyes narrowed, he said, 'Were you hoping this would last longer than a weekend?'

'Oh, now you think I'm here to trap you?'

'I don't know what the hell to think!'

If anything, Costa dared not think too hard. Because suddenly it wasn't Mary's sexual inexperience that was the issue, it was these damn feelings that were getting in the way. The same feelings that had been getting in his meticulously planned way since he had first laid eyes on this woman who had introduced herself as 'Mary from London'.

'I don't want to get involved with anyone,' he told her as they arrived back at the villa.

'So you've said. Several times.'

'And we're too involved already.'

'Hardly...' Mary refuted.

'Yes, we are,' Costa said. 'Look, I don't want the responsibility of a relationship and this is starting to look like one.' He hoped it was too honestly said to sound selfish. 'I don't want all the panic of one.'

'Panic…?' She frowned.

'Wrong word.' He corrected his English. 'Drama.' Then he corrected the situation. 'Look, whether Yolanda believed us or not doesn't matter,' he said. 'She's just going to have to deal with the fact when I tell her that we broke up.'

'What will you tell her?'

'The truth.' Costa looked at her then. 'That we are completely incompatible.'

He'd expected pleas and protests, and yet Costa was coming to understand that he had absolutely no clue when it came to Mary.

She said nothing.

'I'll arrange the helicopter in the morning. I can book a hotel for you in Athens.'

He didn't quite know how to handle her silence.

'You can raid the minibar and go crazy again.'

He found her continued silence unsettling.

'Mary, you really don't need to be sleeping with the likes of me.'

'Save the pep talk,' Mary snapped. 'Believe me, I've been sent away before there was time to unpack more times than you can count. I don't need to be told again that I'm just "not quite right", that I "just don't fit".'

There were no tears and no trace of bitterness in her voice, but then she asked a question.

'You'd really prefer me to have no feelings for you?'

'So you do have feelings?' he demanded.

'Of course I do,' Mary said. 'I'd be crazy to be

here otherwise. But you're right—we are completely incompatible. I would never want a real relationship with you. I want a man who sends cards and flowers and balloons...'

'What *is* your obsession with balloons...?' He screwed up his nose.

'I happen to love them. And you're right. I don't want cold sex and no conversation. I just wanted to play at a relationship and practise on you...'

'Practise?'

'Yes,' she admitted. 'I wanted fun in the sun and to make love and laugh and be close to someone—even if just for a couple of nights. But now one of those nights is about to be wasted in the guest room. Guess what, Costa? I won't be creeping into your room in the middle of the night. I've been lonely nearly my whole life; one more night is neither here nor there. Nor will I be raiding the minibar in Athens. I'll be going out clubbing...' She glared at him. 'I'm going to have some of that cold, meaningless sex you so clearly endorse. *Gia parti mou!*'

'Are you finished?'

'No,' she said. 'I'll be gone in the morning, and I'm guessing you'll be conveniently out, so I'll tell you a few home truths now. Your mother would have loved a card from you...'

He moved his shoulders in a silent, mirthless laugh.

'Oh, yes, she would—and also she'd like to know what the hell happened to your face…'

'She doesn't need to know about Ridge—' He couldn't even finish saying the man's name.

'Just tell her you got into a fight with the guy who was making me miserable. I can assure you she's imagining far worse.'

'Have you quite finished?'

'No! I would have been brilliant,' she said. 'I would have been the best fake girlfriend ever! *I'm* not the one who's struggling to keep up my end of the deal. *You're* the coward, Costa. *You're* the one who refuses to let loose, even for one weekend.'

He said nothing.

'I wish you well,' Mary said, and headed into the guest room. *'Adio.'*

CHAPTER TEN

EVEN THE PLAYBOY doesn't want you... Mary taunted herself as she stripped off and sat on the lonely bed.

She looked through the menu, but it was all dreadfully healthy. Well, it was a health retreat after all. But then she flicked to the late-night menu, and it seemed that from eleven at night until five in the morning some of the guests caved.

There were hot chips and luxurious-looking burgers and *souvlakis*, as well as *sokolatopita*, which Mary read was an old-fashioned Greek chocolate cake, best served with vanilla ice cream.

Oh, my.

Except her stomach didn't growl; it was lower down that she ached. And though she was all wound up from their row, and all churned up at being sent away, thoughts of Costa still brought in new feelings.

Her breasts hurt. Perhaps it was her new Pill, but they felt heavy, and her nipples stung as if they were crying out to be pinched, and her body was all tight and restless.

And on top of all *that* she was sad.

It wasn't just Costa she adored, but Yolanda too. And her party had come to matter to Mary. Now she was about to be put on the next chopper out, and she would never know how Costa had achieved all his business successes, or find out how the party went, or meet poor Roula…

Mary was frantic for some sort of omniscient debriefing, with pie charts and an analysis to fill in all the gaps when it came to this man.

Mary couldn't sleep. She just lay there, wide awake, for hours. And it wasn't just the row, or the fact that she was leaving tomorrow, or the million other reasons that kept her from rest…

She unzipped her bag and took out the little fridge magnet and, as she had on so many nights in a new and unfamiliar place, she decided it needed to be on the fridge.

Except, for all the luxury of her guest suite there was no fridge.

But then, why would there be, when there was natural spring water in a stone jug by the bed and bountiful supplies outside in the kitchen? And there was a fleet of staff a mere phone call away to cater to her every last whim.

Mary cast her eyes around for anything metal that would suffice for tonight, but there was nothing.

'Oh, Mum,' Mary whispered, 'what have I done?'

She waited for the inexplicable comfort of her mum's gentle smile and the comfort she needed.

But for some reason it didn't come. Possibly her mum was cross at her daughter's wayward venture. Or maybe she just preferred to be surveying things from a fridge!

And so Mary lay there in the bed. It wasn't that she was afraid to get up, even though she knew Costa was angry. She'd felt no fear, even when they'd fought.

She was just sad that she was being sent away in the morning, and it was torture recalling the feel of his body pressed to hers and the bliss of his deep kiss…and knowing she would never have it again.

Hearing movement, she sat up. There was the sound of windows and doors being closed and then the little glass window above her door went dark and she realised the lights were all off. There was some more movement as, better late than never, Costa Leventis took his grumpy self to bed.

She waited a full fifteen minutes and then wrapped a towel around her and stepped out quietly, determined to get her magnet safely in place on the fridge in the kitchen and to have it down again by dawn.

'Oh!' Mary exclaimed when she passed a large sofa and saw that Costa was half sitting and half stretched out there, with his hands behind his head.

He hadn't been closing the doors; he'd been opening them up, she realised, as a gentle breeze dusted her skin and the salty scent of the ocean reached her. It was almost as if they were outside.

'I thought you'd gone to bed.'

Costa, who felt not a single need to justify his movements to her, barely glanced up as she padded past towards his kitchen.

Deliberately so.

Mary Jones would not manipulate him.

Except he could see her in his peripheral vision, and when he briefly closed his eyes he saw only the image of her gliding past him again and again.

'I won't disturb you,' Mary said, even as she did just that.

She was at the fridge now and, unlike Costa, clearly felt the need to justify her every movement and share her every random thought.

'I'm just putting my magnet up.'

'Help yourself,' Costa said.

'It goes everywhere with me. I can't sleep otherwise.'

He said nothing to her rather odd statement, even if he was a little curious. Costa could stonewall better than most and simply refused to engage. It was possibly safer.

But though he continued to gaze out to the yachts beyond, and the incredible night sky, still the image of her slender frame moving past him played over in his mind. Like a little ethereal being, she was so pale, and she had made no real noise as she'd slipped out of the guest room and glided by.

Well, until she spoke.

And now she was back in his line of vision, and he felt like a teenager, growing suddenly hard. So, as he had back then, he thought of the boats coming in and piles of fish being tipped out, waiting for him to gut them.

That worked.

'I'm ordering some food,' Mary said.

'Go for it,' Costa said, still refusing to look at her. But then came the prickle of conscience, for she was a guest in his home and had not eaten. 'Seriously,' he said, making the mistake of meeting her eyes, 'whatever you want, just order it…'

His disgusting fish thoughts that had never yet failed him were letting him down now. Or rather, *not* letting him down, he thought wryly. Meeting Mary's gaze had made him acutely aware of the feeling of her novice hand on him, and he lived the moment again.

Go to bed, he wanted to say. *Just… Go. To. Bed.*

But it would seem Mary had more random thoughts that she cared to share. 'I thought I might get a *souvlaki*, and I want to try the chocolate cake…'

'Get whatever the hell you want!'

He saw the press of her lips as she closed them, and the flash of her eyes as his words silenced her, and then she flounced off.

If she was upset, then it would serve her well—to remind her of the emotional desert she was dealing with.

Costa ran his tongue over his new crown and felt the itch of his stitches. That worked better to *let him down* than his stupid fish thoughts.

He wished he'd never laid eyes on Mary Jones.

Liar!

His conscience, which rarely put in an appearance, seemed to have taken the microphone and challenged him loudly, as if on Surround Sound.

Well, then, he wished he'd just said his piece to Ridgemont that night and walked the hell away.

No, you don't.

Okay! Costa silently submitted a final amendment for his conscience to consider. He wished he'd sent Ridgemont off, as he had done, then said goodnight to Mary outside the restaurant and never looked up from his phone as she teetered unsteadily away.

That seemed to silence his conscience.

In fact, the pounding in his head was easing a bit, and the carousel of his thoughts was slowing down.

The *grylo* were loud tonight—or the crickets, as Mary would say. They chirruped outside the window, and though he tried to train his hearing towards the soothing swoosh of the ocean, really it was trained entirely on the guest suite.

He might as well have his ear to her door, for he was straining to hear her.

And it was her silence that killed him as he sat there.

It was her *lack* of tears that burrowed into his cold black heart.

She'd almost cried earlier tonight, though—he was sure of that.

Costa stood, walking over to the fridge to see what she'd been doing. He looked at the odd magnet that now clung to the gleaming appliance and thought of all the places it must have been and all the things it must have witnessed.

Adrift.

Maybe he needed that moment in a debriefing room, with pie charts and markers and such, because he still had questions for Mary.

He knocked and entered and there she stood, phone in one hand, late-night menu in the other, completely naked.

Costa loved it that she did not reach for a towel, just stared at him.

'Have you ordered?' he asked.

Mary was amazed that she could stand nude and make conversation about such an everyday thing.

'I was about to.' She swallowed. 'Do you want me to order for you?'

'Put down the phone, Mary.'

'Am I to receive another lecture?'

'No,' Costa said. 'What was it that upset you this evening?'

'I have to choose one thing?' She widened her eyes. 'Why, Costa, there were so many…'

'Mary,' Costa said, and they both knew the moment to which he was referring, 'you almost cried.'

'No.' She shrugged and lied right to his face. 'I didn't.'

'Mary?'

She could tell him to get out and she knew he'd go. But there was no point in lying now. She stood naked before him, yet he'd invited her to shed so much more than just her clothes.

'Will you tell me about yourself?' Mary asked.

'No.'

He was at least honest about his inability to share, she thought.

'I don't want to let anyone in.'

'That's not very fair.'

He didn't respond to her statement.

'You *can* tell me,' he said.

Could she?

Her mind darted in search of reasons, yet there was no reason she could discover to keep her secret now—no job to lose, no people to offend. She had already seen to that.

'I lied.'

'We all do.'

'I'm not an orphan,' Mary told him. 'I didn't deserve Yolanda's hug. My father is in prison. I visit him every week.' She gave a tight smile.

'He is the commitment that kept you in London?'

Mary nodded. 'He was drunk at the wheel in the car accident that killed my mother.'

'How old were you?'

'Seven,' she said. 'The day of my diving adventure.'

'And he's still in prison?'

'Not for that; the judge gave him a suspended sentence,' Mary said. 'But he'd borrowed a lot to pay the lawyers and I had to move schools. Then something happened at work, and that was the first time he was put away...'

'What about your other family?'

'My granny cut him off,' Mary said. 'I don't know if she meant to, or if she was just angry, but then she died and it was foster homes...' She didn't know what else to say. 'He used to be wonderful,' she added. 'Mr Sensible, we called him. Even though I see him every week, I miss him...'

Mary got her hug then. It was scented in Yolanda's new perfume and it was so nice to be in another person's arms, just to be honest while being held, but still she would not cry.

That she would do next week, and alone, when they'd parted. For now, she just burrowed in his arms.

'I'm so lonely, Costa,' she admitted, and her admission was raw. She didn't even temper her words.

'I don't expect you to get it. I know you're an empty tap where emotion's concerned…'

'Thanks,' said the man who held her.

And although she was pressed against him, and naked, there was no need for his trusty fish method. This was no sensual moment. It was about comfort. And so he held her as her sadness seeped into his marrow.

'I didn't come with you to Anapliró looking for a relationship,' Mary told him. 'I wanted to be part of a family, I guess…just for a weekend.' She inhaled deeper. 'I wasn't acting…'

'I know you weren't.'

Costa sighed, because though she might have been hiding for a long time, he'd been witness to the real Mary.

'Insatiable,' he said, and he was still not talking about sex.

'Yes.' She nodded. 'I actually want to go over to your mother's tomorrow and find out her secret recipe for baclava and make it with her…'

She was honest…so honest, he thought.

'I want to go to the party and dance and then be carried home and made love to.'

'And you want to take her a card signed from Mary and Costa…?'

'Wrong.'

He instinctively knew she was speaking the truth.

'Just from Mary. I bought some seashell earrings

at Thira airport…but they're probably touristy and not to her taste.'

'Who knows with Yolanda?'

'And I know you've got something fantastic lined up for her on Sunday and that I'm not a part of that.' She peeled herself off him. 'I just wanted to play families for a while, and then, believe it or not, I wanted to get on with my life.'

'I see that now.'

'What about you?' Mary asked.

'Me?'

He knew she was waiting for the mystery of Costa to be revealed.

But there were no reciprocal rights with Costa.

He remained closed.

'I've booked your helicopter for ten,' he told her, 'and a hotel room with the best view of the Acropolis.'

'You're very nice to break up with,' she said, then hastily added, 'Not that this was a relationship or anything.'

'Correct.' Costa nodded, and waited for the winds of relief to blow, and yet the air in the room was still.

'I need to eat…' Mary said.

He heard a slight husk in her voice and she cleared her throat.

'I'm starving,' she said as she finally picked up a towel and covered herself.

He saw a speckle of red on her cheeks and some mottling on her chest.

'There is one thing you ought to know,' Costa said. 'Even a slut like me would never have put you in danger.'

'Sorry about that.' Mary winced. 'I was just…'

'I get that you were cross. So was I… But with myself.'

He wanted to touch the little goosebumps on her bare arm, and he could see, even beneath the thick towel, the jut of her nipples. He should walk out through that door right now.

'I've never had unprotected sex,' he told her.

'Bravo!' Mary said, and she saw his odd smile. 'Round of applause for Costa…'

She'd clap, except she was clinging onto the towel.

How, she wondered, could she be naked and relaxed in his arms one moment, and the next be standing feet apart from him wrapped in a towel and about to combust?

'You'd have been fine,' he told her.

'Good to know,' Mary said.

'You *would* be fine.'

She swallowed and, although he just stood there, it would seem it was not just she who was tipping.

She dared not look down to see whether he was as physically affected as she was. In fact, she didn't need to, for his eyes were black with

desire. His mouth was neither smiling nor stern.
It was closed, as though to hold in the words he
wanted to say.

She would have to come to him, Costa had said.
Clearly he was sticking to his earlier promise…

'I'm going to bed,' he told her, hoping like hell she
would join him.

The helicopter was booked, and tomorrow she
would be gone, but now—here—there was simply
no denying their desire for each other.

One night.

It sounded a whole lot safer than two.

So turn and go, Costa told himself.

Except her slender shoulders sagged and he saw
a flash of hopelessness in her eyes.

It was no longer for Mary to come to him,
Costa knew.

She wanted to be wanted.

She *needed* to be wanted.

'Are you coming?' he asked, and saw the shine
of her smile and heard her shriek of delight which
made him laugh as he crossed the room and
scooped her up.

Oh, he was gorgeous… She just clung to his neck
and felt a lovely rush of air as the towel fell away.

As he carried her towards the coveted navy bed,
he asked only once. 'Sure?'

'You know I am.'

She felt the softness of the velvet as he dropped her onto his bed, and then, like some magician, he pulled the velvet from beneath her so that she lay on a cool sheet.

She truly felt as if she was strapped in for a ride on a rollercoaster. A cocktail of desire and nervousness flooded through her as she watched Costa undress. He undressed more slowly than last time, for he was assessing her with his eyes. Of course it was mutual, because that delicious body was being revealed to her again, only this time in a slow, teasing fashion.

She looked at his long arms and his broad shoulders as he stripped off his shirt and was surprised when she saw the little mark that she knew she had made. It made her stomach clench. She felt Costa's eyes move there. Then they moved further down, and she could feel him looking at her blonde curls.

Mary looked up. 'They wanted to wax it all off,' she told him, 'at the salon on Thira.'

Costa told her what they could do with their suggestion and chased away the last whispers of that awful morning.

Although Mary would do it all again just for this moment.

Costa stood, stripped, and this time she saw not a rigid jutting, like before, but instead a soft lifting swell that made her hands want to bunch up the sheet beneath her. He was more beautiful than she knew what to do with and her eyes rose to his.

She trusted him. Costa knew it. And for once someone else's trust didn't terrify him. He didn't feel that this trust came with the usual weight of responsibility.

'I wish I had a phone to take a picture,' Mary admitted, 'so I could look at you again.'

'I swear to God...'

He would warn her later, but for now he shelved the lecture and smiled, because all it was, was bedroom talk.

He saw the leap of her pulse in her throat and then his eyes moved down to her breasts. He wanted to kiss every inch of that skin, or perhaps moisten her with his tongue and stretch her with the caress of his fingers...

Mary watched him harden and felt an urge to raise her knees and open herself to him. It was instinct, but she felt it deep within her.

Costa turned sideways and she saw his lovely bottom, which was rather hairy too, and then he turned off the light so that they were bathed in pale light from the moon. He climbed into bed. He pulled up the sheet and covered them both, and then turned her to face him.

She stared back at him as he brushed her hair

from her face, and then he kissed her cheek, her nose, and finally her lips.

'Better?' he said, and she nodded.

Who kisses like this? Costa thought ages later, when the moon had given up and taken itself behind a cloud.

'Those magazines were wrong,' she said after a while, drawing circles on his chest and then kissing him again. 'You're a very considerate lover.'

'I haven't loved you yet,' Costa said.

And while he knew he should perhaps amend his words, he didn't wish them unsaid. He had already made it clear that this night was a one-off.

They kissed again, little wet kisses that were gentle and tender. The slip of his tongue was like nectar, and his unshaven face was scratchy and nice, and she lingered on the feast of his mouth: deep kisses that were hard, dirty kisses that made her shiver at the suggestions his tongue made, and soft, slow kisses that gently pulled her back.

His hand on her breast was so light at first that it seemed like the barest brush of pleasure. Then his palm rubbed her breast a little harder and he kissed her deeply, while coaxing her nipple to impossible lengths.

Mary was boiling, the sheet suddenly too warm. She wanted to kick it off, but she loved their haven.

His hand found hers and he guided it down until

she held him. Wrapping her fingers around him felt incredible. So incredible. To her surprise, a bead of moisture came to her palm.

His kiss was hungrier now, and he was pulling her hard against his flesh, pressing them together while his leg trapped her. She was now far too hot, and she wanted his hand to touch her where she ached, except he did not oblige.

Suddenly she was frantic, making noises into his mouth before she went rigid, and then began to pulse as she climaxed in his arms...

She was disorientated as he rolled her onto her back, wildly flinging pillows to the floor. His weight on top of her was deliciously oppressive, the crush of his kiss the sweetest reward, and she dragged in air as he lifted himself onto his forearms.

She wanted him heavy on her again, but instead his hand moved between her legs as he parted her thighs and lifted one of her knees a fraction. He was looking right at her in a silent request, and she moved her other leg to match so she was open to him.

She knew he did not need to test with his hand whether she was ready because they were both heady with musky dampness. She felt the head of him sliding back and forth over her heat, before pressing, nudging against the ache that craved him. He kept teasing that pearl with his tip, and then moving back to her entrance while she awaited the inevitable pain, the slow push and the tender squeeze of him as he stretched her.

But then she thought she might faint, for he simply took her. Just seared in all at once.

Not *simply*.

He felt the tear of her virgin flesh and then how tight she was, how she held him inside.

So much for going slowly!

He let out a hollow shout.

It was too intense, too much sensation all at once.

For Costa, the world turned black. He was fighting to give her time to adjust to him. He was over her, panting and trying not to thrust. He was almost braced for a slap, for a shove, for a warning flash from those sparkling eyes. But instead her eyes opened to him, and there was a slight pout to her lips as she smiled.

It was a smile she had never given before…a smile from her that he had never seen…and it invited him to begin taking long, slow thrusts.

'That hurt…' she whispered as he started to move.

'I know.'

'I came when you kissed me…' Mary told him.

'Shh…' he said.

'Why?'

'Because I'm trying not to—'

'Please…'

Costa gave in then, and stopped trying to slow himself down. Instead, he took her with an energy she devoured, for she was clinging onto his shoulders, coiling her legs around him, lost in his power and the sensations of the moment.

Mary felt as if she were being lifted, wrapped and indulged, consumed. His muscles were taut beneath her fingers, and she slipped her hands down and felt his ribs, moved to his hips, and then she pressed them into the buttocks she'd gazed upon before he'd turned off the light. She licked his chest as it moved over her, tasting him.

She wanted to lift her head, but her neck would not co-operate, and she lay in a sudden hush, broken only by the sounds of Costa's effort as he drove into her again and again.

There was a flush of excitement flooding her, a sudden rush sweeping up and down. Costa shouted as if to warn her, to alert her, maybe, for it was as if the gates had suddenly flown open in a storm. He finally shot into her, and she met him and matched his final thrusts. She had not been expecting to shatter so completely. She was trying to twist, to escape this most intense of pleasures, but she finally succumbed, letting the bliss wash over her.

She knew the world would look different on the other side.

CHAPTER ELEVEN

So MUCH FOR keeping things simple!

Costa liked the feel of her tucked into him, the tickle of each breath on his chest and the complete chaos of the bed.

They were still knotted together, and he had salvaged one pillow for his head. His chest sufficed for Mary's. The velvet coverlet was nowhere to be seen, the top sheet was long gone, and they lay wrapped in a bottom sheet.

A gentle knock at the door told him the maid was here with breakfast, and he called through the door for it to be left in the dining area.

'Kalimera.' Mary smiled up at him.

'Correct.' He smiled too.

'Only because I heard you calling out to the maid.'

'Tee kanis?' Costa asked, and watched her frown as she tried to make out his words.

'I know that one…'

It meant *How are you?*

Mary answered him in English. 'I'm very well, thank you.'

'You're sure?'

'Completely.'

'No regrets?'

'None.' Mary shook her head. 'Not one single one. Well, I wish I'd had the chocolate cake, maybe...'

He laughed. 'There will be plenty tonight,' he said, and he stretched over her to reach for the phone. 'I'll cancel the pilot and...'

'No.' It was Mary who stopped him. 'Please don't do that.'

'Why not?' Costa said. 'I thought you wanted to go to a party...'

'I do.'

'You can spend the day at the salon...'

'What else will I do?' Mary asked, and looked up at him.

And Costa, who had been about to guide her hand down and show her what else, knew he'd better be more cautious with his response. 'What do *you* want to do, Mary?'

'I want to know about you, spend time with you, talk to you—all the things you hate.'

'There's no point.'

'Why?'

'You know we're going nowhere.'

'I do know that,' she said, 'but I'm tired of sitting in salons.'

'Then we'll spend the day in bed.'

'I actually want a little conversation either

side of being—' She stopped herself. 'I think it best I leave…'

'Of course.'

She climbed out of bed and knelt down to go through her cases, and he saw his own handprint on the inside of one thigh, pink from their coupling.

He'd cupped her in his palm afterwards, Costa recalled, as she headed to the shower. Mary was right to leave, he conceded, for last night they had crossed a line.

Not sexually. Costa had no issue with crossing lines there, and last night had, by his usual standards, been tame. Yet he felt as if he had taken a blindfold off, and was surveying the damage after some wild misadventure.

And then he recalled his own words.

I haven't loved you yet.

Costa swore!

Three times in a row, he cussed himself.

And then he dragged in a breath as he heard the shower taps close.

He padded out and poured them both coffee. He ate a pastry while doing so, then brought the cups and a plate and got back into bed.

'There,' he said, when she came out dressed in a tiny bikini. She looked utterly perfect, all trace of the night gone. 'Some coffee.'

'No, thanks.' Mary left the bedroom and eyed the breakfast selection. She poured some juice instead, then stuffed some cheese into a bread roll and stood in his lounge eating it.

Last night had been more magical than she'd dared to dream and she did not want the memory of it destroyed. But it was part of a deal she could no longer keep, and she tried to work out how to say goodbye.

And smile.

And not cry.

Oh, she'd done this so many times growing up. She should be an expert.

She swallowed the bread, gulped down her juice and took a breath before heading back to the navy bedroom.

Go, girl!

'The helicopter's at ten?' Mary checked, as if she were ascertaining the time of the next bus.

'Correct,' he said, as she went to her bag and took out some suntan cream.

'Well, I'm going to have a lovely hour at the beach, and then Athens here I come… I shall be raiding the minibar and staying in,' she said, and smiled, because she would be sleeping alone for a very long time—however many decades it took her heart to process him. 'So I hope you really have booked me a room with a gorgeous view.'

'I don't get you, Mary. Everything that we agreed to…'

'Has changed,' Mary stated.

'Because of what happened here…?' He gestured to the disaster of his bed.

'No, because of what happened there…' She pointed to the guestroom. 'I told you my truth and it was wonderful not to be scorned or laughed at or looked down on.' She rubbed cream into her calves as she spoke. 'If you can't reciprocate then that's that.'

She pulled on an oversized sundress—the one thing of her own she had brought to the island—a gorgeous floppy hat, thanks to Leo, and the sunglasses which she'd bought during her splurge at the airport.

'You look very English.' Costa smiled reluctantly.

'Because I am.'

'You really want to go?'

'Yes.' She gave him a half-smile. 'Thank you for the most wonderful night. I honestly mean that. And, please, give my love to Yolanda…'

'She'll be upset.'

'Please!' Mary snorted as she squeezed out a dollop more cream. 'The locals will be waving flags when you turn up alone. I'm sure you can handle them.'

Only it wasn't the locals or tonight that was suddenly on his mind. It was Mary, who seemed happy to chat as she rubbed cream into the backs of her thighs.

'You don't need all that sunscreen,' he snapped.

'Yes, I do.'

'It's early morning and not even summer.'

'I burn easily.' Mary shrugged.

'You don't, though.'

'I'm very fair,' she refuted.

'You're tougher than you look, Mary…' And he was *not* talking about the spring sun. 'You can be anything you want…'

'I hope to be,' Mary said. 'Will you be gone when I get back?'

'I have to go and get a shave and get my stitches taken out…' He stopped then, for they did not require the details of each other's day. 'Yes.'

So this was it.

Mary looked at Costa, all sulky in bed, and wished she could join him. She wished she could suspend her heart for thirty-six more hours. But it was already killing her to leave.

She really had been practising her Greek, and had chosen the farewell that she hoped best fit.

'Sto kaló!'

Costa just lay there as she said it. Not *Goodbye*, nor *See you soon*, or *We'll speak again*. Instead she was wishing him well, or rather telling him *Go to a good place*.

'You too,' he told her.

'Mary?' he called her back. 'There's something for you in the top drawer…'

'What?'

'I got you a phone. You'll need one if you're looking for work.'

'Wow!' Mary said, without her usual enthusiasm. She didn't even open the drawer to look. 'Thank you, I guess.'

He could breathe now that she'd gone. Except there was a gentler farewell too, a more affectionate one, that might have been more fitting, but he dared not use it. And there was still the sweet scent of coconut sunscreen, and when he topped up his coffee he saw that her magnet was still on the fridge.

Costa did admire her.

He might have said it a touch sarcastically last night, yet now, as he wandered to the windows and stood there watching her walk on his private stretch of beach, he realised he really did admire her.

Her hat was being used to collect shells, and she was lost in her own world rather than glancing anxiously back to his. She sought her own happiness and made it herself.

Mary had been planning on changing her life long before he'd come along. This weekend had merely expedited things—and, although he might not recommend her methods for securing it, who the hell didn't want sex?

She had taken off the loose white dress now and was venturing into the water. He was tempted to stand like a lifeguard and ensure she was safe as she ventured out. His concern was merited, Costa told himself, given that she couldn't swim.

But she was just splashing in the shallows, watching the surf and enjoying the day. Then she moved a little further out, testing the water.

The water was bliss.

It was cool on her sex, where it stung a tiny bit, but then all pain just faded away.

The water was so clear that Mary could see little coloured fish darting about, and she was waist-deep now. She felt a ledge of sand beneath her feet and, unsure of the depth, just stood there, lost in her thoughts. Because she was here, and she was sad, so sad, to be leaving far too soon.

But as she scooped water into her hands she knew that whether it was today, tomorrow or next year, it would always kill her to leave.

Not the water, nor the luxury or the beauty…it would kill her to leave *him*.

And then there was movement, a splash, the rush of approach and the wild thrill of surprise. It was so sudden she could not turn round, so exhilarating that there was no time to scream, for she was being scooped up in his arms and he was carrying her out.

'Costa…'

She found her voice and felt his hot skin, the energy of his strong body and the sudden, unexpected joy of the moment. He lifted her high and then threw her into the waves. The water engulfed her, but all she felt was joy returning to her veins and the pumping of a happy heart and the sound of laughter.

'What was that?' she asked as he caught her wrists and dragged her, breathless, towards him.

'I couldn't resist.'

They stood facing each other, smiling, and then he heard the helicopter buzzing overhead.

'I want you there tonight,' he admitted. 'So that you get your party.'

And if that meant sharing his life with her, just for a short while, it was a price he found he was more than willing to pay.

They played some more in the water. He put her up on his shoulders and she said she felt as if she was on the top of the world. They kissed in the water, like true lovers, and then, sandy and wet, headed back to the villa.

'We'll go up to the hills,' Costa said, but she'd stopped in her stride, because Nemo was there.

'I don't want him driving us,' she said.

'No, no,' Costa said. 'He's here to collect your cases. I'll tell him it was a mix-up.'

Nemo did not seem best pleased by the news, and shot her a look before sauntering off.

'Have you told the helicopter pilot?' she asked.

'I'll do so now,' Costa told her. He was about to suggest she put on some shorts, but she looked so happy in her casual loose sundress that he didn't want to. 'Come on.'

They took one of the hotel scooters—a mode of transport that Costa knew well.

'Don't we need helmets?' Mary asked.

'I don't even think they exist in Anapliró...' He shook his head and laughed, but then he saw her expression.

And in that moment something changed in him. *Everything* changed.

'I'll find some.'

They put on their helmets and she clung to his bare back as they zipped along the ocean road. It was an experience she would never forget. He took the mountain route and they climbed higher, to where the air was cooler, with spectacular views of the bay spread out beneath them. He pulled over and they stared down on a *theatron*.

'Galen and I would train there,' he said, 'to get fit for the military.'

'Can we go down there?'

'No time.'

They zoomed off again and she was breathless from sheer happiness. Though she knew next to nothing about him, there was such a sense of freedom and promise in the air as he took her hand.

'Our latest rival,' Costa said as he pulled in at a restaurant. 'Come on.'

'We're not suitably dressed,' Mary said, although that hadn't stopped him. 'They're busy,'

The staff were dashing around everywhere, even though there were no customers, but it soon transpired that they were getting ready for tonight.

A harried-looking chef came out. 'Costa Leventis?'

It was clear they had not met before, and they chatted for a moment before the chef headed off.

'I told him we want to sample tonight's food,' said Costa. 'He's packing a basket…'

'A picnic?'

'Yes.'

'Your *yaya* lived up here?'

'A little further up,' Costa told her. 'That is where we are headed.'

The chef returned with a picnic box, which Costa strapped to the back of the scooter. They both got on after expressing their thanks, and they carried on up the mountain.

It took another fifteen minutes or so and then he turned off onto a small road which Mary noticed was freshly paved. Costa halted the scooter and she watched as gates opened on their approach.

Mary was confused. Hadn't he grown up poor? This was as lush as any villa at the retreat, and the gardens were vast and beautifully planted.

'Where are we?' Mary asked.

'This is my mother's gift for tomorrow,' Costa explained. 'If you knew the hell I've gone through o keep this secret…' he explained. 'Roula is the only one who knows.'

Bloody Roula, Mary thought.

'Let's go and see…' He took out some keys and unlocked the door.

They walked through the cool villa, which was a mixture of old and new. Antique ornaments sat next to a gorgeous picture of Yolanda on the beach, laughing as she caught a wave. And on the white mantelpiece were smiling photos—some of Costa. He had been a big baby, and that made Mary smile. There were also pictures of a younger Yolanda with friends.

'Are there any of your father?'

'Yolanda would just smash them. I don't have many good memories of my father.' He put his arm around her. 'You have some good ones of yours, though.'

'I do…' Mary nodded. She was starting to remember them now. It felt as if this short time away, the space to breathe, was allowing her to look back on things differently. 'He was always so together; now he's just a shell.'

'Poor man,' Costa said.

She had never heard anyone speak of her father with empathy, let alone kindness, and it made her feel a little muddled as they headed outside and sat by a stream.

The air was so fresh and clear and they could see for miles—the azure ocean below, and the retreat,

and the tiny white puffs of cloud that were burning off even as she gazed up at them.

'Eat,' Costa said. 'Here's your chocolate cake...

There was *soumatha* to drink—an almond syrup
topped with icy sparkling water—and so many del-
icacies to try. Mary looked over to Costa and knew
that even with the pain of the goodbye to follow
this would always be the best day of her life.

For now Costa let her in...

'There are a few main families on the island.'
He pointed his finger to the expanse that stretched
around and beneath them. 'The Kyrios family way
over there. Then the Drakos family have some of
the western shore.' He pointed towards the village.
'The Barios family.' He guided her to the thick trees
behind the retreat. 'That land was owned by the
Hatzis family.' Then he tapped the ground. 'Here
and some of the shore was Argyros. There were
others, but those five had most of the land. It was
worth nothing then. Oh, and Jimmy had the hotel,
but he's gone now.'

'Jimmy?'

'Came here for a holiday and never left.'

'What about the Leventis family?' Mary asked.

He shook his head. 'The only thing they owned
was a poor reputation. They moved to the main-
land long ago, but my father returned on occasion.
He was a drifter,' Costa explained. 'But my mother
was Yolanda Argyros and got into trouble at fif-

teen—that trouble being him…and subsequently me. There was a lot of pressure on them to marry.'

'From her parents?'

'From everyone. I think he tried to settle. He worked over on Santorini,' Costa said. 'And he made some good money for a while—at least by Anapliró standards. He took the ferry each morning, but then he started to forget to come home one too many nights. Still, that secret stayed in the family. My *yaya* was a mean-spirited woman,' he told her. 'She punished my mother and shamed her.'

'For getting pregnant?'

'For that, and for her husband leaving, for being ill, for needing medicine… She choked on a chicken bone a couple of years back, thank God, or she'd have lived to be a hundred.'

'Costa!'

'What?' he said. 'I'm cold because I don't pretend to love someone who didn't deserve it?'

'No…' She didn't know what to say. She did not want half-truths, or for him to feel he had to hide anything from her.

'I worked hard…got lots of jobs. I made sure my mother always had her medicine, and every six months I got her to Athens to see a specialist.'

'How?'

'Catching fish, gutting fish, selling fish…' He didn't tell her how the fishermen had at first laughed at the skinny kid who had pleaded for work. 'I loved night fishing, and those men turned out to be the best teachers. At night we would listen to the laughter carrying from the parties on the yachts, where they were all deciding our fate…' He saw her frown. 'Someone developing the island was just a matter of time. We all knew it. "You should be at those parties, Costa," they would say to me. I told them I intended to be.'

He lay back and she sat still, just watching him thinking.

'You can't just rock up, though,' Costa said. 'Everyone aboard is vetted. You have to be seriously rich or, if you're just a worker, you have to sign NDAs.'

'Were you a worker?' Mary asked, her throat feeling tight.

He shook his head, 'No. I worked in the restaurant kitchens in Santorini and then I would sleep on the beach and be up for when the night boats came in. I would hose down the rich men's yachts too. There was no chance of getting on them, but I was always listening. Then I came out of the army and I was hot.'

'But not modest?'

'No,' he said. 'There was no time to be. Galen and I got office space in Athens and I worked it on the islands. I didn't have much money, but I looked good and some owners paid me to eat in their restaurants, go to their clubs…' He looked up. 'The right ones.'

'I've never been to a club.'

'Stay out of the ones I went to, because in your case they'd be the wrong ones.'

'Leo said you wore his designs?'

'Yes. I wore smart clothes, showed them off to the necessary people, got to know them. I always knew the island's potential, but I also knew that in the wrong hands it could be destroyed by too many footsteps. I had a couple of bits of land by then, bought for loose change, really, and most of the locals trusted me. I had a share in Jimmy's bar, I had this land—not in my name yet, but it was in my family…' He looked at Mary. 'And I had anger fuelling me.'

She sighed. 'That's a terrible source of fuel.'

'Not always,' he disagreed. 'I knew where I was headed and I worked on getting there. I dated a woman who had access to some information.'

'Were you using her?'

'She was forty. I was just out of the military, not even twenty, and wearing Leo's designs.' He shrugged. 'We were using each other, I guess. She finally got me into a party I wanted to go to. I knew Ridgemont would be there. He called the island a slag heap—as you well know.'

Mary nodded, forgetting her chocolate cake.

'"Yes," I agreed, "it's a slag heap." Then he told me about the "peasants", who wanted too much for their land. I agreed with him again, pretended I'd blown far too much on it already.' He gave her the tiniest wink. 'But…'

'But?'

'That's it. Time to party.'

She pressed into his side, prodding him for more, but he just laughed and pulled her down to him. 'Seriously… Two weeks later he put in a high offer to the Hatzises for their land, but I already owned their shed…'

'So they couldn't sell?'

'No—and anyway, they trusted me. Mary, I opened Ridgemont's letter of offer to them. We were all laughing.'

He pulled her onto his stomach and she looked down at him.

'Same with Jimmy. We got so wasted that night…' He looked up at her and slid her down. 'That bar, it was on the exact spot where you lost your virginity, Mary.'

'Wow.' She was stroking the little hairs on his stomach and then she asked, 'And the Kyrios family?'

'They always held out for more. They still do,' Costa said. 'It didn't matter in the end. I wanted this side of the island the most.'

Suddenly he was tired of talking and perhaps she sensed it, for he felt her hands move down.

He watched as she took him out and then he looked up at her, at her mouth and the tentative lick of her lips. 'Go on.'

'I don't know how.'

'There's no rush. Just begin, and it will all go from there.'

Costa wanted this the most now.

CHAPTER TWELVE

'FIVE MINUTES!' CALLED Mary as she dashed in from a *very* last-minute appointment at the salon.

Costa was standing by the glass doors, and not even the Aegean Sea, glittering behind him in all its splendour, could draw her attention, for he was beyond beautiful.

He wore black trousers and a white fitted shirt that showed him off to perfection. He was for the first time clean-shaven, his hair tidy and brushed back to give full access to his stunning features.

Mary had met him first in a high-end restaurant, but that had been just one version of him.

This one she was struggling acutely with.

This potent version of Costa she did not quite know how to handle. Because she was expected to dance with him, and kiss him, as if it was normal for them to do so, and yet all she wanted to do was shed her clothes and run to him.

'You've shaved,' Mary said, impressed with her only slightly high tone.

'I've *been* shaved,' he corrected.

There was something else, though. It was as if he'd spent the entire day being polished and perfected, when in fact they'd been beyond late getting back to the retreat.

'You're ready?' she asked.

'Apart from my watch…'

'You'd better find it, then. I won't be long.'

'No rush.'

He poured her a glass of sparkling water and handed it to her. Mary almost didn't want to take it, for she feared she might spark into flames if he touched her.

'Thank you,' Mary said, and took her drink into the bedroom. Except he followed her in and stood in the doorway. He seemed to think they would chat as she selected her underwear.

'It's from Leo's summer range,' Mary said as she tried to wrestle her body into the tiniest panties. 'It's called Hope Dies Tonight! What a dreadful name.' He said nothing. 'Apparently,' she rattled on, as she snapped on her tiny bra, 'it sounds better in Greek.'

'I don't know about that,' Costa said. 'It certainly looks better in English.'

Mary looked down. There was clearly no safe flesh-coloured underwear in Leo Arati's range; this set had a shimmer about it, to cover the most private parts, but it still left a lot exposed through the mesh fabric. Frankly, the Deception range would have been safer!

He watched her wrestle with shoes, and then he took her lovely pale gold dress and held it out for her.

'Costa…' It would be easier for her to dress alone than to lean on his shoulder as she stepped into it. Her desire, now discovered and unleashed, should have been pleased to lie quiet for a while and rest, yet it felt as if it was ready to leap into action at the merest whisper of encouragement.

She loved his deep kiss on her stomach as he pulled the dress up, and the way he stared right at her as he tied the halter neck, and the heat of his hands as he reached around to cup her breasts. She wanted him all over again.

'I can't believe I'm saying this,' Mary muttered, 'but I don't want to go to the party…'

'We need to go now.'

He had turned her on to the nth degree and now he wanted them to go to his family party?

He looked at his wrist, where his watch should be but wasn't. Was he finally relaxing? Finally letting go? But he just collected the card, signed by Mary, and the little present.

She'd make him pay for teasing her like this later!

This time they walked hand in hand through the balmy night, and stopped for a kiss just before they went in. It was sheer bliss.

The second she stepped through the gates she saw thousands of candles almost drowned out by a full moon, the glitter of an ancient pool, and people. People, food and the throb of music. She couldn't wait to explore.

'Costa! Mary!' Yolanda waved them over and greeted them with a smile. 'You both look stunning.'

'You look beautiful too,' Mary said. 'Your dress…'

'Leo, of course,' Yolanda said, and then looked to her son. 'I wanted to wear Yaya's earrings; they would have been perfect. But I must have misplaced them…'

'You don't need them with that dress.'

'Really?'

He was so kind to her, Mary thought. Even if he didn't want to be here, no one would be able to tell.

'I'll give you your gift tomorrow,' Costa said. 'On your actual birthday.'

'Spoilsport.' Yolanda pouted.

'For now,' Costa said as he handed over Mary's card.

Yolanda was, as Mary had predicted, delighted. 'Eyelashes!'

'They peel off,' Mary explained.

Yolanda also loved her seashell earrings—well, perhaps not the actual earrings, but she greatly appreciated the gesture.

'Finally.' She patted her son's smooth cheek. 'And your stitches are out…'

Mary looked over, for she realised she hadn't

even noticed. Perhaps that was what was so different about Costa tonight.

'Tell me, please,' Yolanda persisted. 'What happened?'

'Leave it…' He went to pull Yolanda's hand away and then changed his mind. 'It was the man who was making Mary so miserable. He was waiting for me at the airport.'

'Ha!' Yolanda's eyes widened and then she laughed. 'One minute a fighter, the next in a helmet on his scooter…'

Costa rolled his eyes.

'They're all laughing.' She looked over to Mary. 'Well done, you. I have told him more than a million times.'

And as Yolanda introduced Mary to the nearest group of guests, Costa's hand snaked naturally around her waist.

She felt his warm palm sit loosely there, and was so aware of his touch. It struck her as odd that something so simple could cause her stomach to tighten low down, as if a clock were being wound too tight. She had to force herself to focus on the introductions.

'This is Mia…' Yolanda said. 'The retreat's chef who is refusing to eat…'

Even the sulking Mia smiled. 'Because *I* wanted to cook for you tonight.'

'You cook for me every night,' Yolanda said.

'I hear you visited the new restaurant today.' Mia

fired a look at Costa. 'When you haven't even been into the retreat's restaurant.'

'Because I save the best till last.' Costa smiled.

He was different here, Mary realised. He was lighter here. Perhaps because it was his home.

'Roula…' said Yolanda, and waved her over.

Mary braced herself for impact. But Roula was not what Mary had expected. Though seriously beautiful, it was as if she was doing her best to hide the fact. Aside from the diamond clip holding her heavy Titian fringe back, Roula was very conservatively dressed, and still wore her wedding ring.

'Mary…' Roula hugged her. 'Oh, my God, finally he brings a woman home, and of course she is beautiful.'

There was not even a fish bone's worth of contention that Mary could detect, but all eyes were on them. All eyes!

It was as if the entire party were watching this moment, as if all the guests were collectively holding their breaths. Mary felt as if she'd walked in halfway through a complicated stage play. No, not even halfway through…more like at the curtain call.

These were the people who played the biggest parts in Costa's life and somehow she was trying to work out their roles. Roula was supposed to be the leading lady tonight, and Mary felt as if she had stepped into her shoes at the last minute and bumped Roula down to a supporting role.

'This is my brother Nemo,' Roula said. 'Though I suppose you will already have met…'

'We have.' Mary smiled. 'He picked us up from the ferry.'

'Always working.' Nemo's smile did not reach his eyes. 'It's good to see you both.'

It was the perfect party, Mary thought, although there were no balloons. But there was laughter and dancing and incredible food that she barely tasted, for she'd been eating on and off all day. This was the kind of night Mary had always wanted— a glimpse of family and acceptance, and a lot of dancing and conversation.

'I have no idea what Costa is up to tomorrow,' Yolanda said as the men all began to dance in an odd circle. 'Do you?'

'I would never spoil a surprise,' Mary answered carefully.

She watched Costa slip away from the circle and glance over to Roula. Mary felt a dip in her stomach as the pair moved away together for a moment.

No!

He had told her they were friends, and she had believed him, but, yes, a little seed of doubt sprouted.

Stop it now, Mary told herself as Costa came back from wherever he had been with Roula. *This is not your life.*

And then glasses started clinking and it was time

for the speeches—except Yolanda really didn't seem to want that.

'I'll keep it short,' Yolanda said, 'because my English is not good enough for a long speech, and I want to welcome Costa's English friend. Really, thank you all for being here tonight. I was twenty-five when Stavros left. Two weeks later I lost my sight, I lost my dignity, but worse than that I lost my hope. I thought my life was over. Twenty-five years later, life has never felt so good...' She looked over to her son. 'I love you, Costa.'

It was the shortest, sweetest speech, and Mary's mind was darting. Twenty-five years ago meant Costa had been ten! Ten! Working at the marina, while also being a provider and carer for his mother.

His English hadn't slipped when he'd described love as 'panic', because Mary was doing that even thinking about what he must have been through.

It was all a blur after that, really. Costa made a quick toast to his mother's health, but Yolanda *really* did not want any more speeches and soon the party was back in full swing.

And she was in Costa's arms again. But there was a churning of anger growing within her.

'Some lucky star,' Mary said, and she had to swallow down her bitterness. Only it coursed through her even while his hands held her steady. 'You never said you were so young. Sleeping on a beach...' She was trying not to imagine the horrors.

'Mary,' he said, 'nothing terrible happened to

me. Yes, it was difficult, and it was a challenge, but nothing truly bad happened.'

She looked up.

'I do believe I was always looked after.'

They swayed, and danced, and yet she could not close her eyes and sink into the bliss, for she was suddenly aware that she was leaving tomorrow and did not quite know how to step away as she had promised.

Mary looked at the candles burning down, and before her very eyes one died and sputtered out. She watched the snake of black smoke and she repeated over and over to herself the very wish made on the night they had met, *Please don't let this man see how I feel.*

Her eyes drifted as they danced.

Nemo clearly wasn't off duty. He was standing watching proceedings, ensuring there was no trouble. His eyes landed briefly on Mary and she stilled.

'What's wrong?' Costa asked.

'Nothing.'

He ran warm hands down her shivering arms. 'Tell me.'

'Nemo,' she said. 'I don't think he likes me…'

'Forget it,' Costa said, and held her closer.

Mary fought to get back to being fine.

But Costa had been right: she *was* a liar—because she wanted more than a weekend. She wanted to demand to know where the hell he and Roula had disappeared to. She wanted to command him never to let her go, to let her stay with him always.

She couldn't help herself. 'Where were you and Roula…?'

'I wanted her to speak with Mia, and arrange to take up champagne and some food to get the house ready for Yolanda tomorrow. Why?'

'I just wondered…'

It would have to do. For now, for tomorrow, for ever.

And if the moon and the stars would just hold their place, if the music would never stop, then they might never have to move on from this moment.

CHAPTER THIRTEEN

THE FALSE SUMMER was over.

Mary woke to a day on Anapliró that was silvery grey and yet still exquisite.

She could see the beautiful sea churning from where she lay. She and Costa were spooned into each other, and possibly, Mary decided, she had played the part of fake girlfriend a little too well, for he was trying to justify why he couldn't take her with him.

'I would ask you to come today,' Costa said, 'but I need to speak to Yolanda away from here.'

'Of course.' She tried to pull her lips into a smile, even though she was facing away from him. 'That's for the two of you. I understand.'

'Even so…'

'Hey, you promised me Sunday off,' Mary said.

He rolled away and onto his back as she reminded him of all they had agreed to.

'I want to go and look at the shops…' She turned and moved towards him, looking him square in the eye as she lied. 'And I want—'

'I get it… I get it. You're fine with the arrangement.'

He showered and dressed, and only when he had left to collect Yolanda did she let her smile fade.

How was she supposed to leave someone she loved? Did she wave, or smile, or did she just make it easier on her heart and disappear now? Take the ferry to Thira, maybe? Just be gone?

It seemed rude, but somehow kinder to her heart.

The coffee was strong, but nothing could clear the mist in her head.

Mary started to pack, but though she had done that more times than she could begin to count, this time it was agony. It was like trying to squeeze her heart into the case, and she was sitting there defeated, nowhere near packed, when there was a knock at the door.

He'd come back, she thought, with a surge of delight, and she almost ran to the door naked. But then, realising Yolanda might be there with him, she pulled on a wrap and flung open the door.

'Nemo?' She frowned, for he stood there in his uniform with a female security guard at his side.

'This is my colleague,' Nemo said, as she met his blank brown eyes. 'There have been complaints of things going missing.'

'I'm sorry?' Mary shook her head. 'We haven't had any trouble. At least—'

'Since you arrived,' Nemo cut in. 'I need to check your things.'

'No!' Mary went to close the door, but his foot moved to halt it. 'You can wait until Costa is back,' she told him.

'Yolanda has asked me to do this while her son is with her. We have spoken and she is aware now that you are here as a working girl. I can either do this discreetly or I can call for the police.'

It was the ultimate walk of shame. Walking into the room alongside two security guards who knew that Costa had paid for her services. But far worse than that was the fact that Yolanda knew.

Except it wasn't really like that.

Was it?

The only vindication was that of course she wasn't the thief.

Still, it felt nerve-racking.

The luggage that Costa had bought her was all clear.

'I told you,' she said.

Then they went through her make-up bag, and it was then that Mary knew she would be leaving right away. There was no way she could stay here a moment longer after this.

But then Nemo opened up her folded hat, which was still in the wardrobe, and shook out the shells she had collected form the beach. Onto the bed fell some earrings, then a watch, and a silver hairpin with a diamond as big as Mary's little fingernail…

'No!' she said immediately. 'I did not take them.'

'So they just fell into the hat?'

'Of course not.' Mary could feel her heart thumping in her chest as her worst nightmare came true. 'I would never...'

She would not even pick up so much as a penny on the street to avoid precisely this situation. Her father's crimes tortured her still.

'It's a set-up.'

'What the hell's going on?'

It was Costa, with his mother behind him.

'Oh, Mary...' Yolanda said.

The shell earrings Mary had given her were dangling on her ears and so it hurt even more that her voice was wretched with disappointment as she surveyed the bed.

'Papou's watch, Yaya's earrings...' Yolanda started to cry. 'That is the hairclip poor Roula lost last night.'

'Get out!' Costa said.

Mary stilled at the darkness in his voice, but it was aimed at the guards.

'I mean it,' he said. There was no doubting that he did. 'Out.'

'Do you want the police?' Nemo asked from the safety of the doorway.

Costa told him once again, this time somewhat less than politely, to leave.

'Send a car.' Yolanda dragged herself into management mode. 'No police.'

'You too,' Costa said to his mother when the guards had departed. 'Go.'

'Costa, listen to me. We have policies for this.'

'I'll wheel you out myself,' Costa warned.

Mary stood silently, like a statue, barely able to breathe as Yolanda turned to leave.

'Costa…' she tried one last time.

Mary turned and saw that Yolanda was crying and couldn't manage the door. In silence he went over and saw her out.

'She broke down in tears halfway up the mountain and told me what was happening back here,' Costa explained when he returned to the bedroom, his face the colour of putty. 'Things going missing, Nemo ran a background check…'

'But I have no background.'

He just stood there.

'Costa…' She took a breath. 'You know I've never slept with anyone else and you know I'd never steal.'

He would not even attempt to unscramble that one. He was cross, for there was drama, and there was panic, and all of this he most definitely did not want.

He had flown down that hill in a fury when Yolanda had confessed, and still he could not catch his breath…

'We could have met when the ancient civilisations built that pool and I still would not have worked you out by now.'

He looked at the bed and the jewels and the

watch and the shells and the scatter of sand. He was cross still, but for different reasons than he'd expected.

'Surely you could have come to me if you needed more?'

But Mary clearly had more important things than money on her mind and she snapped, 'How does Yolanda know about our agreement?' She felt ill at the very thought.

'I don't know.'

He surveyed her half-packed cases and figured she'd been about to do a runner with the items. He thought of the plans he'd had for tonight and suddenly felt like the biggest fool who'd ever lived.

'You were clearly about to leave.'

'Yes.' She was all shrivelled up inside again; all the confidence she had found had simply evaporated, but there was anger brewing too.

The injustice of it all! Costa stood, watching, as she started to put the rest of her things in her case. She did not cry, nor try to defend herself. Instead, her face was pinched, and he felt sideswiped again.

Because instead of feeling his usual world-weary indifference, he was crushed. He couldn't summon up an angry word, nor bear to see her out to the car.

Costa took hold of her shoulders. 'Mary, listen…'

He had never felt this close to anyone—never wanted to be this close to anyone…never been so desperate not to lose someone… He had never had to ask a woman to stay in his life. Usually he was the one ensuring they would leave as soon as possible.

'Look, I'm not going to lose you over Yaya's earrings. She was a miserable old cow…'

Not going to lose her? *What was he talking about?*

She was shaking now with anger and shame. 'We can get past this,' he told her.

'Your mother won't.'

'I love her, but I long ago stopped answering to her. All that matters is us and that I forgive you,'

'How generous of you,' Mary sneered.

'What the hell?'

What had he done wrong now? Because whatever it was she was shaking off his touch and pulling on her clothes.

'I'm telling you that we can get past it, that—'

'I don't need you to forgive me, Costa.' He watched her snarl. 'I needed you to believe me. I *slept* with you…'

She said it as if it mattered. and it did—it had—but she upended his brain and shook the contents out, and he struggled to hold on to logic as she continued.

'I slept with you, but more than that I gave you my heart. I was absolutely prepared for it to be broken, absolutely prepared to walk away as per our agreement, but never like this…' She was closing up her luggage. 'You should have believed in me…'

'You make no sense.' He just could not see it. 'I

know you are struggling. I have struggled too, in the past, and I am saying that I understand.'

'You don't,' Mary retorted. 'I am always the first one they point the finger at.'

'They?' Costa reared. 'Who is *they*?'

'At school, at work, in the foster homes I was sent to. It was always easier to blame Mary Jones. *"Her dad's in prison and she's always short of money. Oh, and she's a bit odd, you know."'*

'And Mary Jones lies,' Costa pointed out. 'An awful lot.'

'Yes,' Mary said. 'But I told you how much it hurt me to lie to your mother and to you. You should have stood up for me, defended me.'

'Mary…' he said as the retreat's car arrived. 'Barely a word you've said since we met has been true…and now, when it suits you, I'm supposed to believe you're telling the truth?'

'I haven't told you anything. You never even asked. But, yes.' She nodded. 'Hell, yes.'

Let her go, Costa told himself. *Let Mary from London, with her penchant for kleptomania, get the hell out and let me return to my life.*

Except he liked it better with her here.

'Mary…' He watched her stomp angrily out to the car. Of course members of the security team were there, and no doubt his mother was watching too.

God, he loathed it here at times.

He almost charged out to haul her back, to halt

her and have a good old row with her. But then for the first time in his life Costa Leventis froze.

Because he *did* believe in her. And he hadn't even asked her… Even if it defied logic, he absolutely did.

His guts turned to ice.

Costa called to the driver to wait, went inside and grabbed a package, then walked back to the car and knocked on the rear window. She ignored it, but the driver knew who was boss and the rear window slid down.

'Here.' He emptied his wallet of notes and dropped them into her lap. 'You might need—'

His lips pressed into a grim smile as the notes fluttered back and drifted off to the pool as she refused to accept them.

'Don't throw this back,' he said. 'You need a phone.' He dropped the one he had bought her into her lap and thankfully she didn't fling it back. 'I'll call you.'

'Please don't.'

'Na proséhis.' This time he used the more fitting farewell. *Take care. In the process.* Yet her little phrase book might not capture the true affection behind the term.

And then she was gone.

CHAPTER FOURTEEN

'I'M SORRY, DAD.' Mary pushed out a smile. 'About last week.'

'It's fine, Mary. They got a message to me and I've always said you don't have to come every week.' He looked at her. 'You've got a suntan…'

Mary felt more wretched with each passing day, yet somehow she looked healthy and glowing.

'Yes,' Mary said, and took a breath. Certainly she didn't want to tell her father about her weekend. But… 'Actually, I do have some news…'

She'd been using the phone Costa had given her. She loved it, actually, and had learnt from some friendly backpackers at the hostel she was staying in how to set it up. And how to recognise and block calls from Greece!

'I've got some interviews lined up,' she told her dad.

Except her father didn't want to hear about her work.

'You've been crying.'

'I haven't.'

She didn't exactly sob herself to sleep in the dorm at the hostel, but she'd had a little weep this morning when all the excited tourists had headed off. She'd thought she had been so careful, but obviously he had spotted her slightly puffy eyes.

'I've got hay fever.'

'Mary. You might be able to fool everyone else, but I'm still your father...'

'Just leave it, please, Dad.' She looked at the bleak surroundings and then swallowed as her father pushed a parcel towards her. 'What's this?'

'It's okay, I've got permission. I'm sorry that it wasn't ready in time. It was in the kiln. I made it for your twenty-first.'

'I thought you'd forgotten.'

'Of course not. I was just embarrassed that I didn't have anything to give you, so I just...'

Avoided it.

They were both brilliant at that.

It was a little dish painted in her favourite colours, all oranges and bright blues. It almost looked as if it belonged on Anapliró.

'It's beautiful,' Mary said.

And now the tears did fall—not a lot, but a couple of hot salty ones squeezed out of her eyes and ran down her cheeks.

'You can use it for your earrings and things...'

A bitter laugh shot out of her lips and she quickly looked to her father. 'That wasn't aimed at you. This really is gorgeous...'

And then she looked up and saw his eyes were full of concern, just as they had been when she was a little girl.

Could she tell him?

How?

Yet she ached for advice, for an adult in her life who cared and who took an interest in her.

'I met someone.'

'Costa Leventis?'

'How do you know?'

'Mary, when all the newspapers were asking "Who is she?" I knew the answer. I'm your father. I'd recognise the back of your hand! How did you meet?'

'I was on a date with someone else…' She was too wretched to lie. 'Not a date, exactly.'

'Mary, please don't take that path—'

'I've learnt my lesson,' she interrupted. 'Well, I thought I had. Costa rescued me from an awful dinner. We agreed to spend a weekend on Anapliró—a Greek island,' she explained. 'I know it was a terrible idea, but it honestly didn't feel like that at the time. He's not really close to many people—just his mother—but he's…' How best to describe Costa? 'He's a bit of a lone wolf. Certainly he's not the settling down type. I was supposed to convince his family that he was finally serious about someone. He told me from the start that he didn't want to get involved, except…'

'You've fallen for him?'

'Yes,' Mary said. 'Dreadfully so…' The tears were falling thick and fast now. 'Not that it matters. There's Roula…'

'Roula?'

She shook her head. 'Anyway, he thinks I'm a thief.' She took a breath, because she didn't want to hurt her father, but these were the bald facts. 'Some earrings went missing. They were found amongst my things. A watch too…'

'So he saw you off the island?'

'Not at first.' She let out a low laugh and stared at the tissue she was shredding with her incongruously still gorgeous nails. 'He was all magnanimous and said that he forgave me. That he *forgave* me, Dad—'

'He *forgave* you?' her father cut in.

'I needed him to believe in me.'

'Mary, don't disregard what he did. I'd kill for you to forgive *me*.'

She went very still and carried on staring at her hands, but then she dared to look up and she met his misty eyes.

'I was always so cautious…' her father said.

She wanted to halt him. It hurt too much. But she forced herself to listen.

'Your mother used to tease me about it,' he admitted. 'Sometimes she told me off for being such a stickler for the rules.' He gave a pale smile. 'I said we should get a taxi home.'

'You didn't, though?'

'No.' There was so much regret in his voice that he didn't even need to shake his head to emphasise it.

'What happened?' Mary asked, for the first time.

'It was just a work do.' He shook his head sadly. 'You were upset. It was after that diving incident at school.'

'Yes.'

'I didn't even want to go. I wish to God we never had.'

'Mum wanted to go,' Mary said.

'She did.' He gave a fond smile. 'It turned into fun; she could always light up a room. She wanted to dance, have champagne...'

'Mum was supposed to be driving,' Mary said, recalling her mother picking up the car keys. 'It was decided.'

'Don't...' Her father shook his head.

She remembered scolding Costa. *You shouldn't speak ill of the dead.* And yet by never doing so, by never examining what had happened that night, somehow she had turned her mother into a saint. And this perfect person, her beloved mother, had been so much more than that. She had been funny, loving, mettlesome—and, yes, contrary at times. A perfectly imperfect human whom they had both loved so much.

'You *both* made a terrible mistake that night,' Mary said, and she thought of Costa's words when she'd told him about her father: 'Poor man.' He had shown such compassion.

Forgiveness from someone you cared about was a gift indeed, and she swore to remember that in the future.

For the first time since she was a little girl she took her father's hand. 'She wouldn't want this for you, Dad.'

'I know, and I know I've said it a million times, but I *am* going to sort myself out.'

'You will.' She smiled. 'I know it's taken a long time, but I do forgive you. Both of you,' she added.

'It means the world to hear you say that.'

He seemed to sit a little straighter now, and Mary felt a little less adrift, for it was as if he'd become her daddy again. Mr Sensible.

'You are not to go running off with strangers ever again,' he said.

'I won't.' Mary even smiled at the very notion. 'Costa really was the exception. The first time I saw him it felt as if I'd just recognised a friend.'

But her father was dealing with the practicalities. 'So, this man who by all accounts trusts no one…?'

'What accounts?'

'I do read the papers here, and I can get online too, and when I saw you with him… You're telling me that he forgave you on the spot?'

'But for something I didn't do. He never even *asked* me.'

She remembered Costa glancing at the bed, at

the watch and the jewels, at the evidence glaring him in the face. And he had forgiven her practically instantly.

She thought about him asking his mother and the security guards to leave, remembered the brief flicker of disappointment, and then something else in his eyes: concern. Compassion.

He had forgiven her. And now, as she sat there, she couldn't even call it unwarranted—because that would be to discard an incredibly precious gift.

'Why would he forgive you?' asked her dad.

'I don't know.'

'Don't you think you should maybe find out?'

'It's too late for that.'

Her father smiled then. For the first time in fourteen years Mary saw her father's real smile.

'It's never too late,' he told her. 'I found that out today.'

For once the visit was over too soon, and Mary left with her mind whirring.

Why had Costa so readily forgiven her?

She was frantic to call the retreat and plead with Yolanda for a chance to speak with him. But she'd probably hang up, or get Roula...

She hadn't even reached the prison gates before she'd done a frantic search for airfares on her new phone. Perhaps it was just as well she was broke, or this time tomorrow she could be flying to Athens and sitting outside Costa's office like some crazy stalker...

'Mary?'

She heard her name said in rich, deep tones, as only he could, and thought she must be hearing things. Yet she looked up and there he was.

Dishevelled again, and unshaven.

His eyes were so black he might well have been in another fight—except they looked exhausted rather than damaged.

Mary walked out of the prison and into his arms. Whatever was happening, for a moment she simply relished being held by him, and the delicious safe space that his chest provided.

She could hear the *thud, thud, thud* of his heart. It was faster than she had known it before, even faster than after they'd made love, and yet he stood completely still as she gathered herself together in order to hide the glistening of love in her eyes.

Finally she was able to pull back a touch and ask, 'How did you find me?'

'I ask the questions,' Costa said, looking down at her sternly. 'I spoke with your delightful ex-boss on a couple of occasions last week.'

'With Coral?'

'Yes. You didn't just leave your job to come to the island, did you? You left your home too.'

'It was never really a home.'

'You are dangerous, Mary Jones,' he said, but he smiled along with saying it. 'When you go for something, you really go for it, don't you?'

'It would seem so…' She sighed.

'Well, I have told Coral that I am still deciding whether or not to pursue a course of legal ac—'

'Pursue what?'

'Her treatment of you was so wrong, Mary, and believe me she has been told. Oh, and I can tell you the reason you're getting nowhere with your references. I had Roula call her, and it would seem dear Coral takes less than a minute to discredit you. I thought it would be hard to find out where your father was imprisoned, but Coral sang like a bird.'

'I knew it,' Mary muttered. 'So what *are* you doing here? Apart from making trouble at my old salon.'

'A number of things. But first off I came to apologise.'

'For what?

'For not believing in you. For believing the worst.'

'Costa…' She wanted to interrupt him, to pause, to think over what her father had said, but he shook his head.

'Not here.'

She was shaking as he led her to a car, and bewildered as they were driven to the hotel where they had first met.

Back where they'd started.

They were sitting in gorgeous chesterfields, he with a cognac and she with a hot chocolate, she looking at the purple orchid in its glass jar while he closed his eyes.

But then he pulled himself out of his reverie and opened his eyes, and there was the Costa she knew.

'So, what have you been up to, besides trying to get over me?' he asked.

'Oh, I've been trying to get over you, have I?' He really was *so* arrogant. 'Actually, I've been busy looking for work. And I've got interviews—not just for work. I'm looking into a flat-share with some lovely Belgian people I met in the hostel I'm staying at.'

She deliberately didn't let on about the rather dire status of her emergency fund.

'I owe you some money…' Costa said. 'Kristina said you never gave her your bank details…'

Ah, so *that* was why he was here.

'I don't want your money, Costa. Most of our time together was wonderful. It would cheapen it for me if I was paid. Anyway, you've already given me enough…'

'What?'

'I've got nice clothes for interviews and I've got a phone…' She took a breath. 'I know better now how things should be, how I should expect to be treated. You did that for me, and it's worth a whole lot more than a bundle of cash. I want to think of our weekend as…'

She shrugged and tried to come up with a word that downplayed the true depth of her feelings. Certainly a man like Costa would be bored with women declaring their love for him.

'As a fling.'

'Oh, I think you can do better than that,' Costa said.

She flushed. 'Okay, a *romance* rather than a paid date…'

'Better.' He gave her a small smile. 'Mary, it was a romance.'

'Thank you.' With her father's words still spinning in her head, she knew there was something else that needed to be said. 'And thank you for forgiving me. I'm still furious that you felt you needed to, but I understand what it cost you to do it.'

Costa frowned. 'I don't forgive easily, Mary, but I figured you had your reasons…'

He struggled to elaborate, for the waiter was hovering, and even if this was his chosen secluded spot for business, it felt too exposed for this conversation.

Yet there were things they had to get through, so he nodded for another drink and she declined one.

'You blocked my number,' he accused. 'I bought you a phone and the first thing you learnt was how to block me.'

'I was about to unblock it,' she admitted. 'And if you didn't answer I was going to call your mother, or even Roula, and ask to speak with you…'

'About that…'

He'd closed his eyes again, and Mary had the awful feeling she was about to be told that he had given in to the pressure from his family and his community.

'Here…' He put his hand into his pocket and handed her something precious. 'You forgot your magnet. It didn't exactly suit my fridge…'

She held it as he shredded her heart.

'Roula asked what the hell it was when I invited her over…'

'Spare me the details, Costa.'

'You always said you wanted details, though.'

Yes, she had. And, in truth, she did want the details and so she nodded.

'Do you know why I let you go?' he asked.

'You didn't have any choice,' Mary pointed out.

'Do you know why I wasn't waiting for you in Athens?'

'I never expected you to be…'

'Mary, for a while there I told myself you were a little magpie.'

How did he get away with smiling as he said that?

Except she smiled too. 'I have many issues, Costa, but stealing isn't one of them.'

'Well, whatever your issues, we will get to them later, but I wanted you to leave because I felt you were in danger.'

'Danger?'

'You never liked Nemo.'

'No,' Mary said, 'probably because he didn't like me…' She took a breath. 'I know he's your head of security, and so you must trust him, but I think he set me up.'

'Absolutely he did,' Costa agreed, and then accepted his drink from the waiter. 'Mary, I am going to tell you something that no one knows. Not even my mother—not a soul. It is incredibly important that you don't breathe a word of this.'

'Whom would I tell?' she asked. 'I'm not exactly connected.'

'I know,' he said, 'but this is very delicate. After you left, I took my mother to her new home…'

'Did she love it?'

Costa glanced sharply up.

'Yolanda was a little upset,' he said, and she was sure he was trying to be tactful. 'About the events earlier…'

'I ruined her birthday, then.' Mary sagged in her seat.

'Of course not,' Costa said. 'She blamed me entirely.'

'Well, you will go bringing outsiders home!' Mary sat back and wagged a playful finger, in her endless attempt to hide how much she was hurting.

Just this conversation to get through, she told her weary heart, *and then we can move on.*

Only it wasn't like a prison visit that seemed to stretch on for ever.

It wasn't duty or a sense of responsibility that tethered her to the chair opposite Costa.

It was love.

A different kind of love from any she had known.

A grown-up love that felt rather too enormous to contain.

There was sadness, and longing, but also love.

For though his hands were on the table, she felt as if they were cupping her cheeks again. Or gently holding her hands. Or as if they had crept up her skirt and were lightly stroking her thighs.

Her ache for Costa was permanent, and now heightened by his presence.

'We spoke at length,' Costa said.

'Who did?' Mary asked, because she was looking at the little scar above his eyebrow and trying not to think of those invisible hands.

'Yolanda and I,' he said. 'Are you listening? This is important.'

'Of course.'

'We spoke a lot about days of old, promises made and then broken and the hurt they caused. She's tired,' Costa admitted. 'Tired of working so hard at the retreat, tired of being vigilant…'

'Surely she can slow down now?' Mary frowned.

'She said a few things that troubled me,' Costa admitted. 'Mary, why won't you look at me?'

With supreme effort, she met his eyes.

'Anapliró is not mine,' he said. 'Yes, I own a lot of it, but it has traditions and history that can never belong to one person. She told me of the shame she had felt when the Kyrios family cut us out. Yolanda knew it was not me they spurned, but the burden of caring for her. Some of the family bitterly regret it now. She can feel it. I told you Yolanda was a white witch.'

'You did.' Mary was on the edge of crying. 'How did she find out about our arrangement?'

'Nemo lied. I spoke to him when I got back. He said he had done a background check on you and that's how he got Yolanda to sign off on what he did. I knew for certain then. Mary Jones from London, no fixed address…' He started to laugh, but dryly. 'We're good at the retreat, but we're not MI5. He was lying,' Costa said, and then he offered her a toast and drained the one-hundred-year-old cognac without it touching the sides.

Mary sat bewildered as he righted himself.

'After I spoke with Nemo I found Roula, and asked her to come to dinner at my home…'

'Costa, please…' Mary closed her eyes and massaged her temples. She wanted details, but not those.

'I'm Greek,' he told her. 'I do business face to face. So you will listen.'

'Even difficult business?'

'Especially so.'

She took a breath and forced her game face back on. 'So Roula came for dinner?'

'Yes. You remember Yolanda said that Roula had been upset for a while…?'

Mary nodded.

'We spoke. At first I spoke about the jewels and

the watch her brother had found. She was nervous, I could see, so I changed the subject to work…'

'And drank a little ouzo…?' she said.

'Of course,' he agreed. 'Unlike you, some people need to be a little loose to speak their mind. Roula wants to leave the island. But her family are upset at the thought, and Nemo especially does not want her to leave. He thinks that old promises should be kept. In fact, every day that he works for me he feels is an insult.'

Mary met his eyes urgently and opened her mouth to speak, but he overrode her.

'Listen!' he warned with a pointing of his finger. 'Roula is more than troubled. She found something in her brother's garage and is scared that her husband's death might not have been an accident. I told you about *philotimo*…honour… Well, his is misguided, I believe. He wants the way paved for his sister to marry me and will use any means necessary. He is bitter and twisted and black with silent rage…'

'Oh, God!' It was far worse than she had even considered. She thought of Nemo's cold brown eyes and felt fingers of fear grip her heart. 'Has he been arrested?'

'Not yet.' Costa shook his head. 'I gave him a promotion for catching a thief, but first he's taken a few weeks' bonus vacation…'

'Thanks.'

'No…' He smiled. 'Thank *you*! Look, I can't

have him near any guests. He's being investigated, and I believe he'll be arrested any day now, but it was five years ago that Roula's husband died, so they have to be sure before they make a move. Nemo is in a good mood right now, telling everyone that Roula and I are together. Mary, I had to put that in place before I came here. I want you to—' His voice cracked then, only she knew this was not fear. This was bigger.

'Not here,' he said.

Mary frowned. 'No one can hear.'

'Can we go up to my suite? I can't do this with an audience. Look, I understand if you're not comfortable...'

Mary stood without thinking, then wished she'd remained seated—or hesitated, at least! She was like a puppy galloping towards a treat, she thought angrily. For, despite all promises to her father and to herself never to make foolish mistakes again, Costa seemed to be the exception to her new rule.

She had a vision of him rolling up in London twenty years or so from now, sitting at this table, where she would be waiting for him. He was both her weakness and her strength.

Conflicted, she took his arm and they walked to the elevators.

He was going to tell her he and Roula were engaged—she just knew it.

Yet that lure was still there between them. *Always there.*

She sighed as the lift hurtled them up to his suite.

One more time, perhaps…

One last time with the man she would always love…

They stood on opposite sides of the lift. Costa looked at Mary and saw not the choppy new haircut, nor Leo's stylish clothes, but the little fridge magnet she clutched in her hands.

Her admission of loneliness still humbled him. Her bravery terrified him at times—the fact that she would simply step out, or dive off, or refuse the easy route. And her honesty and loyalty disarmed him a thousand times over.

He was the coward—at least where love was concerned. And it was time now to be brave.

As they reached the penthouse floor he stopped her from stepping out of the lift. 'Do you know why I forgave you when I thought you had stolen those family jewels?'

'No.'

'Because they mattered less than you.'

Mary stilled, unsure where his words were leading, unsure quite what he meant. She was silent more from being overwhelmed than by lack of words, for she was desperate for clarification.

'I figured you had your reasons,' he said eventually.

'I didn't, though…'

'I was hoping we could work it out.'

She frowned.

'Together.'

She stood so still, yet there was absolute movement in her soul. For she felt as if he was stepping into the empty space contained within it.

'You were worth more to me than any jewellery,' Costa told her, and offered his arm again.

On shaky legs Mary walked towards his suite.

'You are the first person since my father whose leaving has mattered.'

They were at his door, but he did not go in.

'I lied too, for I do have some good memories. He taught me to swim, to fish… I loved him. But one day he decided it was all too much and just walked away.'

'I'm so sorry.' She looked into those stunning eyes and the firewall was momentarily down, for there was old pain and confusion swirling there.

And so they just leant on the door, as if they were back lying in the pool, holding on to the edge and floating in the water.

'I love my mother—you know that. But I wanted to be a kid, and a teenager too. I wanted school rather than work—fun rather than the constant fight to make ends meet and to care for her. I wanted liberty and I swore I would get it some day. It has taken me more than two decades to wrestle Anapliró from developers' hands. I did up the family home, and I got that final piece of land back the day before we met. My duty was finally done and I could distance myself some more… I planned to see Yolanda for her appointments in Athens, and such, but I was ready for a life alone—or to be like ships that pass in the night on the occasional visit home.'

'Beholden to no one?'

'Yes,' Costa said. 'But it's more complicated now.'

Of course it was. Yolanda wanted old promises kept and her son close by—and lots of big babies to smother in her love…

Mary knew that could never be for her. And not just because she was an outsider, but because she could never, ever leave her father behind.

'Shall we go in?' he asked.

They were still in the plush corridor, Mary realised. She stepped back from the door they were leaning on and he swiped it with his key card. She knew it would be far wiser to leave now. It bleeped with a red light and Costa swore in Greek.

He seemed… She frowned, because this very assured man seemed nervous as he swiped it again.

And then the door swung open and the very breath was stolen from her throat.

There were balloons.

Hundreds of balloons.

Gold, silver, pink and red, they floated or stood trailing delicate ribbons.

Mary walked through them slowly, looking up, looking around, and fourteen years of missed celebrations were erased.

'Cake!' she croaked.

'*Sokolatopita* on one side,' Costa told her. 'Strawberry Fraisier on the other…'

She had never imagined that he might be so romantic. It had never entered her head that this man could take all the broken pieces of her and knit them together again.

But then smash it all on his inevitable way out…

'I love you,' she told him, and yet she kept her arms by her side. 'But I think you already know that. Please don't take advantage of the fact.'

'Who's taking advantage?'

'You are. You're going to marry Roula and have big, fat babies and live on Anapliró. Well, I won't be your mistress. I can't be!'

'What the hell are you talking about?'

'You'll cheat.'

'I would never cheat.'

'I'll be your London lover, then,' Mary accused. 'You'll roll through the city every now and then and I'll—'

'Seriously,' he said, 'what the hell are you talking about?'

'Costa, why did you bring me up here?'

He looked at her, all flushed and angry—and jealous! Oh, yes, she was!

Costa smiled inwardly at her misunderstanding, but he loved this game too much to concede just yet.

'I want sex.'

He had warned Mary he would be upfront about it

when he asked, and she stood there, surrounded by balloons, watching unmoved as he took his tie off.

And then he shrugged away his jacket.

'Are you going to just stand there?' he asked, thinking of the other time she had stood in his doorway, so innocent yet so utterly brave.

'How dare you? To come here and expect this…to toy with me when I've told you I love you. I can't, Costa. I won't.'

She watched him strip off so easily; he made her weak and so desperate to join him.

'I can't be a mistress or whatever… I can't be lonely any more.'

'Mary, you're never going to be lonely again.'

And at that point she just melted.

One last time and then it would be over.

He kissed her so hard that she saw stars, and her skin screamed for him as he shed her dress.

She had on her Hope Dies Tonight underwear set. Not that she'd ever be wearing it again, for he tore it off.

And she was weak, weak, *weak*. Because she was frantically kissing him back. He tasted of cognac, and decadence, and it was the kiss she wished she'd been able to give him had he taken her to his suite that first night.

It was desperate.

She was scaling his body, clinging to him, and the constant need he created was pounding at her senses.

The low throb of desire that had begun on the night of her birthday had become a constant companion.

He held her hips and one of the balloons popped—or was it her resistance? Because she was sinking onto him, wrapping herself around him.

She bit his shoulder, for it was as if they were back in the pool, or on his dark navy bed, only it didn't hurt this time.

He guided her to a table and placed her hands behind her, so that she held herself up on its edges. Mary arched back, with nothing but the impossible pull of him holding her up. He was watching their rapid union, looking down at where they were joined. The sharp, breathy noises he made as her slippery body writhed in his hands seemed to spur him on, yet he held her steady so he could drive into her.

She wanted to watch him, but her neck was arching back. So she gave in to the delicious sensation. His shout and the way he seemed to swell inside her were both urgent, but she was lost in the abrupt thrusts he delivered, and in his sudden stillness as he drove into her for the final time, holding himself there while he poured himself into her.

And as he cried out she shuddered around him, knowing that nothing would ever be as incredible as this moment right here, right now.

Her arms were trembling and he was stroking her stomach, still shuddering with his last precious drops, and it actually hurt to feel sensation receding.

He scooped her up in his arms and gathered her

close to his cooling body. He carried her to the bed, laying her down and falling on top of her.

They paused for a minute or two, catching their breaths and enjoying the delicious side by side of their bodies.

'You didn't open your present,' he told her in a breathless voice.

'I don't want presents,' she told him.

'Okay,' he said and sat up. 'I'll open it.' He picked up the box and showed her. 'I have very good taste, by the way.'

'Good for you.'

'Platinum,' he said, 'because I don't like gold jewellery. I really do need to lose that watch—God, I wish someone *would* steal it!'

She felt the stretch of a tiny smile, but she did not dare to hook her heart onto his words.

Except…

'I had Leo speak to a local jeweller who *knows*. Because I wanted a sapphire the colour of an Anapliró sky at midday, which is the closest I can get to describing your eyes.' He took her left hand and found her ring finger and said simply, 'I need you to marry me, Mary.'

'Costa…'

'Be with me.'

'But Roula…?'

'We are friends. I have told you that,' he said, but she felt her eyes filling. 'Always just friends…'

'It's not that.' She and her father were finally close again. She could not abandon him now.

'I've spoken to your dad.' Costa's voice slipped into her despair. 'I visited him.'

'You've met him?'

'Yesterday. I asked his permission to marry you.'

Her heart flooded then, because her father had lost so much pride and Costa had given him a piece of that back.

'We spoke about you, about your mother, and I told him about the moment I knew I was in love with you.'

'When?'

'You asked for scooter helmets and I laughed— and then I thought of him, of the agony of playing a part in the death of his wife, in the death of his daughter's mother. I could have taken you up that hill and been every bit reckless as he...'

'No.' She shook her head.

'Yes,' he said. 'Right or wrong, I would never have forgiven myself, and I knew then that even if it went against all my plans to be free, I was in love.'

'And you didn't think to tell me?'

'I didn't know what to do with those feelings,' Costa admitted. 'So I decided to wait until after Yolanda's birthday...maybe in Athens...'

Mary lay there, spinning.

'I didn't tell your father this,' Costa said, 'but that man needs a good lawyer. And whatever happens from here, I shall make sure he gets one.'

'Thank you.'

'I swore him to secrecy.' Costa frowned then, for

ever the cynic. 'You really had no idea I was going to ask you to marry me?'

'None…' Mary blinked. 'I even told him a bit about what had happened. He just asked me why you would forgive me when everything pointed to my guilt.'

'Because I love you first,' Costa said. 'Then we deal with any problems.'

It was a world she'd doubted she would ever know again, and yet since Costa had come into her life she had been right slap-bang in the middle of it.

It was her parents' love that had made her brave as a little girl. It was their love that allowed for risks.

And it was his love, Mary realised, that had coaxed her return.

'I would be beyond happy to marry you,' she told him.

As the cool metal slid onto her finger she felt its weight, and she lifted her hand to stare at the enchanting stone. It was indeed as blue as her eyes and as deep as her soul.

She looked up at Costa, her safe harbour, and her adventure too.

'Can we have babies?' she asked.

He rolled his eyes. 'Yes.'

'And live on Anapliró?'

'We'll go often,' he said. '*Very* often,' he conceded.

'Are you going to call Yolanda and tell her?'

'I'm not that Greek,' Costa said, and he climbed onto the bed to kiss her, and hold her, and who knew what else…? 'It's *our* party.'

EPILOGUE

MARY WOKE ALONE.

Costa was at times surprisingly old-fashioned, and he had insisted they spend the night before their wedding apart.

It was a very tight timeline, and had been kept a huge secret due to all that was transpiring with Nemo. But she refused to think about any of that today.

The wedding would be on Anapliró.

They had planned to hold it in London, but her father's leave to attend hadn't been approved, and so, without him, they had moved the venue.

Costa had flown to Athens yesterday, for dinner with Galen and to tell him about the wedding and ask him to be his best man.

Mary lay in bed and looked at her ring to calm the flutter of panic in her chest. She wasn't nervous about the day ahead—the journey to Anapliró and then to the gorgeous old church—she was excited for all that.

It was leaving London.

Though both Costa and her father had done their best to reassure her, she felt as if she was leaving her father behind. She had visited him yesterday, said her goodbyes, and sworn she'd be back very soon.

Mary climbed out of bed and pulled on a wrap as someone knocked at the door and her breakfast was delivered.

'The hairdresser will be here in thirty minutes,' the butler informed her.

'Thank you.'

It was a *very* tight schedule.

Costa was holding true to his faith, and there were many traditions, yet Mary could not shake the feeling that she was missing one of her own.

More than one.

She missed her mother so badly today.

And her father too.

'Buck up,' she told herself.

After all, she was marrying Costa and all her dreams were coming true.

She reached for her juice and saw that there was a note on the tray. She immediately recognised Costa's thick black scrawl.

To my bride...

This must be a Greek tradition she didn't know about, Mary thought as she sliced open the envelope—the groom must write to his bride on the wedding day. Hopefully Costa wasn't expecting anything from her.

As it turned out, it wasn't a particularly romantic letter.

Dear Mary from London,

After your hair is done, please put on your wedding dress and get ready. I have arranged for a photographer to come to your suite as the wedding album should include you getting ready in your home town.

Costa x

Another bloody tradition she didn't know about.

It was odd, but it upset her that their wedding had turned into a lavish Greek affair.

Actually, that was a lie.

She must stop doing that!

Mary would have paddled herself to Anapliró in a boat just to marry Costa and be surrounded by love.

As her hair was teased into loose waves, Mary knew that what was really upsetting was that, apart from the groom, the people she loved wouldn't be there.

But it would be easy to put on the dress and smile for some photos. Then she smiled for herself, because her dress really was breathtaking.

Designed and handstitched by Leo Arati, it was the most stunning shade of white she had ever seen.

It was a very clear white, but in a certain light there was the palest, palest hint of lavender. She had told him about the lavender in her childhood garden, and Leo had allowed her to take this piece of her home to her wedding.

Her flowers were delivered—a small hand-tied bunch of forget-me-nots with a little sprig of lavender and one single violet orchid... She touched its velvet petal.

All brides cried on their wedding day, Mary told herself, and gave in to a little weeping as she sat there in her dress—even though she was happier than she knew how to be.

She was marrying Costa, Mary told herself, and gazed down at her ring again, which always calmed her.

So much so that she blew her nose and rather wished she did wear make-up, because her eyes were a little bit pink, as was the tip of her nose. Still, she smiled resolutely when the bell to her suite chimed, determined the photographer wouldn't capture her tears.

Except it wasn't the photographer.

'Dad!' She couldn't believe it, but her father stood there, resplendent in a dark suit, with a prison officer a few discreet steps away from him. 'What on earth...?'

'I've got leave for a couple of hours.' Her dad smiled and took in his stunning daughter on her wedding day. 'Oh, Mary...' Now it was her father crying, and he took out a handkerchief and wiped his face. 'You look beautiful.'

'Oh, Dad.'

She could not even attempt to stop her tears from flowing now, and she was just so overwhelmed. But for now she was at least safe in her father's arms.

'Wipe those tears, Mary. We've got a wedding to get to.'

'But I'm getting married in Greece.'

'There's been a change of plan. You're getting your marriage *blessed* in Greece,' her father corrected. 'Costa is waiting downstairs to marry you.'

'He planned this!'

'Yes, but we weren't sure till last night…'

'He's not in Athens, then?'

'He's not.' Her dad smiled. 'I've got something for you…'

He took out a box and she frowned as she opened it, and then blinked in recognition, because it was her mother's pearls.

'I could never sell them,' he said. 'She wore them on our wedding day.'

He helped her put them on, but there was one more thing she needed before taking her father's arm. Mary peeled the little magnet from the fridge and held it in her palm.

She was ready.

Or so she thought.

But as she stepped into a rather lavish room at the hotel, Mary gasped.

Yolanda had flown in for the occasion, and it was as if she had brought Anapliró with her, for she was a swirl of silver and turquoise and she was using all her energy to stand as Mary walked in.

Mary could see Yolanda's tears, and see her hesitancy about what kind of reception she might get. And though Mary wanted to run to Costa, she went to Yolanda first—her soon-to-be mother-in-law.

Costa was standing at the front of the room, staring ahead, and she knew he was allowing his bride this moment to take in the people who were at her wedding, to know the love that surrounded her now. Such love. For as she gave Yolanda a hug she was held in return, and there was the scent of the perfume Mary had bought her.

'I'm so sorry,' Yolanda said. 'I was hurt for Costa…'

'It's fine,' Mary soothed. 'Let us look to the future.'

A very handsome man came over then, only it wasn't her groom, for Costa still stood at the front.

'I'm Galen,' he said, kissing Mary on both cheeks.

Galen was the most handsome robot on earth.

'I never thought I'd be at Costa's wedding,' he said, by way of introduction. 'And I deal in probabilities.'

Mary smiled. 'I'm so glad you're here.'

'It's good to be here.' Galen nodded. 'But we do need to get on.' Then he smiled. *'I ora i kalee…'*

The time is good...best wishes...good luck... She didn't need her translation book to know what he meant.

'Thank you.'

Mary returned to her father's arm and centred herself, puffing out a soft breath as the piano that had been gently playing moved on to Wagner. A Greek celebration and Greek music were all to come, but for now the 'Bridal Chorus' struck its beautiful chords and everyone turned to face her.

But she had eyes only for one person now.

Costa really was tall, and he looked exceptionally so in a dark morning suit and silver tie. He was wearing a single violet orchid in his lapel, and she knew this one she would press and keep for ever. He was so beautiful.

'You shaved,' she said, and her hand moved to his smooth cheek and felt his strong jaw.

'Of course,' he said. 'This is the most important day of my life.'

'Today,' the celebrant said, 'we are here to witness the marriage of Costa and Mary... Who gives this woman?'

'I do,' said her dad, and Mary looked over to see him smiling.

'Thank you,' she said as he let her go with such grace.

And then she listened as Costa gave her his chosen vows.

'I, Costa Stavros Leventis...'

She smiled for she hadn't known his middle name until this moment.

'…promise to love you and be there for you always. To debate at times, perhaps…' he smiled '…but always from a place of love. That will never change.'

It was overwhelming and it was wonderful to have his love offered so freely. It was precious too, and for a moment she wondered if it was possible to be this happy. She feared she might wake up and find him gone.

Except his olive hands held her pale shaking ones firmly.

'I, Mary Elizabeth…' She could barely get the words out she was shaking so much.

Costa steadied her with his warm touch and she fingered the little magnet she carried in her hand, so that it felt surely as if her mother smiled and gave her blessing.

'Take your time,' he whispered.

She nodded, and took a breath, for there was just one promise to make, just one promise to keep… 'I, Mary Elizabeth Jones, will love you for the rest of my life and beyond.'

'We're good to go, then,' he said as he slipped on the ring. 'I'm going to kiss you now, Mary Leventis.'

No longer adrift, she stepped into his arms and Costa kissed his beautiful bride.

'I can't wait to take you home.'

* * * * *